CW00819683

Mama's Rules

THE DEVIL'S HANDMAIDENS MC: ATLANTIC CITY, NJ CHAPTER

ANDI RHODES

BLUE JOURNEY PUBLISHING

Copyright © 2023 by Andi Rhodes

All rights reserved.

No part of this book may be reproduced in any form or by any electronic or mechanical means, including information storage and retrieval systems, without written permission from the author, except for the use of brief quotations in a book review.

Cover Artwork - © Dez Purington at Pretty in Ink Creations

For all the people who have found a once in a lifetime love more than once. You are incredibly lucky!

And for those who have yet to find it… don't worry, you will. You just have to remain open to possibility.

And remember, love and hate are often two sides of the same coin.

Also by Andi Rhodes

Broken Rebel Brotherhood

Broken Souls

Broken Innocence

Broken Boundaries

Broken Rebel Brotherhood: Complete Series Box set

Broken Rebel Brotherhood: Next Generation

Broken Hearts

Broken Wings

Broken Mind

Bastards and Badges

Stark Revenge

Slade's Fall

Jett's Guard

Soulless Kings MC

Fender

Joker

Piston

Greaser

Riker

Trainwreck

Squirrel

Gibson

Flash

Royal

Satan's Legacy MC

Snow's Angel

Toga's Demons

Magic's Torment

Duck's Salvation

Dip's Flame

Devil's Handmaidens MC

Harlow's Gamble

Peppermint's Twist

Mama's Rules

Valhalla Rising MC

Viking

Mayhem Makers

Forever Savage

Saints Purgatory MC

Unholy Soul

A note from the author

Y'all, human trafficking is real. Trauma is real. This book is not. It is fiction and should be read as such. I'm not, nor am I trying to be, an expert on how human trafficking survivors behave or react once they return home.

If you can read this with an open mind, and set aside preconceived notions, or even facts if you know them, then enjoy! If not, this book probably isn't for you.

Happy reading!

Andi

Mama...

I don't have much in this world beyond The Devil's Handmaidens MC, and I've always been okay with that. My sisters are my life, our mission my reason for being. But that all changes when a little boy chooses me to be his protector, to be his voice.

When I take him home, my plan is to drop him off and get out of dodge. Unfortunately, I'm met with a father who doesn't know how to drag himself out of the pits of Hell. And for some reason beyond my understanding, I want to help. I just have to convince the man, and my club, that I can.

But helping them isn't the only problem I'm facing. No, I also have to help stop the new threat to the club and community, all the while protecting the boy and the man I'm coming to regard as family.

Benson...

Losing my wife was the hardest thing I've ever had to deal with in my life. At least, until the day my son was kidnapped. When the police came up against dead end after dead end, I thought he was lost forever. My world became a black hole I couldn't escape from.

I drown myself in booze, every day trying to numb the pain of my new hellish existence. It never works, but my heart doesn't seem to care. That is, until a woman shows up on my doorstep, with my son in tow. I know I need to be the father my son deserves, but it's not easy. And it's made harder when the woman insists on helping because she makes me want more than to simply get better. She makes me want to be the man I thought was long dead.

When evil reappears, threatens to destroy the new life I'm building, can I keep those I love safe, or will the bad guys win again?

Devil's Handmaidens MC is a multi-author world focusing on a badass all-female MC with various chapters/locations written by some of your favorite MC authors.

Prologue

BENSON

"I DON'T WANNA GO IN."

I force a smile and kneel so I'm eye level with my son. At seven, Simon isn't the happy-go-lucky little boy he was six months ago. When Katie, his mom and my wife, died, he started to morph into a kid I barely recognize. To be fair, I'm probably not the dad I was, but life will do that to a person.

"I know you don't, kiddo," I say as I lift the strap of his backpack onto his shoulder. "But ya gotta go to school. We can't stay home forever."

He frowns. "Are you gonna go to your new job?"

I would if I'd found one.

A month after Katie died, I lost my job. We moved a few weeks after that, and I told Simon it was so we could have a fresh start. The truth is, no one wanted to hire the depressed widower who never comes to work and snaps at anyone who tries to talk to him. Moving to Philadelphia was necessary if I'm going to find employment.

And if it comes down to it, we're now close enough to my brother that I can go work for him if I have to.

"Of course I am." The cheer in my tone rings false, but if

my son notices, he doesn't say anything. "It's a big day for both of us, huh?"

Simon nods, but his frown remains in place. "I don't know anyone here, Dad," he laments. "What if the other kids don't like me?"

Simon has always made friends easily, so I'm not worried about his ability to win the other kids over.

"Don't like you?" I ruffle his hair. "Kiddo, everyone likes you. And you'll make friends in no time."

"You'll make friends too, Daddy," he tells me as his gaze slides to the elementary school building.

Out of the mouths of babes.

"C'mon," I urge as I stand and grab his hand. "You've got this."

Simon lets me lead him to the door, and he doesn't let go until we step inside. I walk with him to the school office, where we're greeted with enthusiasm and smiles. Ten minutes later, Simon is seated at a desk in his new classroom, and I'm staring through the small window, unable to tear my gaze away from my little boy.

"He'll be okay."

I glance at the principal, who escorted us to the room. She's a kind woman who clearly loves her job.

"I know," I mutter, shoving my hands in my pockets. "It's just…"

She rests her hand on my arm. "I understand you've both suffered a great loss recently. I'm very sorry about that, but Simon needs this. Normalcy will help him."

Huffing out a breath, I chuckle. "Normalcy. I don't know what that is anymore."

"Mr. Green, have you or Simon received any counseling?"

I turn away from the window and stare at her. If I had a nickel for every time someone suggested counseling since Katie's death, I'd be a rich man.

"I'd be happy to recommend several in the area," she adds.

Clearing my throat, I rock back on my heels. "I appreciate that. But we're fine."

She nods. "Okay. But if you chan—"

"I'll be back at two-thirty to pick up Simon," I say flatly and turn to walk away.

As I stride down the hall toward the exit, I can feel the principal's eyes boring a hole into my back. I wish I could say she's being judgmental because that would make it easier to hate her for thinking she knows what's best for me and my son. But I can't say that because all I feel in her stare is concern and… pity.

The sun beats down on my face as I stroll to my truck, and once I'm in the driver's seat, I lean my head back.

"Aw, Katie," I mumble as tears fill my eyes. "I fucking miss you."

There's no response, not that I expected one. She's dead after all. But once, just once, it'd be nice to feel like she's with me, like she's watching over me and our son.

The rest of the day goes by in a blur. I spend a few hours job-searching and submitting my resume to contractors in the area. I've always been good with my hands and building houses is where I shine. Or I did… before.

When I can't take the sound of my own thoughts any longer, I grab a beer from the fridge in our small two-bedroom house. I twist the cap off and toss it in the trash before flopping down on the couch and chugging. It doesn't shut off my brain, so I close my eyes and silently beg for sleep. At least in my dreams, I can pretend that Katie is alive.

I wake up a few hours later and panic when I see that I'm late to pick up Simon. Rushing to the elementary school, I mentally prepare the lie I'm going to tell him as to why he had to wait for me.

But I'm never given the chance to tell the lie because when I arrive, Simon is nowhere to be found, and my world stops turning for the second time in six months.

CHAPTER 1

Mama

ONE MONTH LATER...

"WHAT CRAWLED UP YOUR ASS?"

I whirl around and glare at Giggles, the club's road captain. My fingers tighten around the handle of the ax I have raised above my head as my heart continues to pound. I've been at the targets for the last few hours, needing to burn off some steam after our last rescue mission.

"How are you so fucking calm?" I snap, rage threatening to burn me from the inside out.

Giggles eyes my ax before skirting around me to sit on the bench. She stares at me for a few seconds and then heaves a sigh.

"I'm not calm, Mama," she says. "It's taking everything in me not to ride out of here and search until we find those kids. But what good would that do? We have all our resources focused on the search. I have to trust that we'll find them, otherwise, I'd go... crazy."

I shake my head. "But what about Noah?"

At the mention of her little brother, her eyes narrow. "What about him?"

"Doesn't it scare you that there are monsters in the world, that he could be in danger?"

"Every fucking second of every fucking day." Giggles shrugs. "What we do, what we see… it eats at me, reminds me that no one is safe. But I can't let Noah see that, see my fear, because then he'd be scared, and that's no way for a little boy to live. Noah deserves to be happy and carefree. So I do my best to make sure he is."

"I don't know how you do it. I'd have Noah locked up in a padded room where nothing and no one could touch him."

Giggles laughs, but I fail to see the humor. "No, you wouldn't." She stands. "Look, we were too late today, I get that. But there's always tomorrow."

I turn and launch my ax at the target. My chest heaves, and tears prick my eyes. What the fuck is wrong with me? I'm normally able to distance myself from the Devil's Handmaidens' work to rescue human trafficking victims. I have to be able to in order to stay sane. But I'm not feeling very sane right now.

"Tomorrow is too late," I snark. "You know as well as I do that a buyer can one-click at any time."

We all thought that taking down the Ricci Crime Family would give us some breathing room, but almost immediately, another trafficker set up shop in Atlantic City. You'd think we'd know by now that bad guys don't take a break, they don't quit.

Which means, neither do we. And I'm tired. So goddamn tired of humanity sucking giant donkey balls.

"Sounds to me like you're giving up," Giggles accuses, and I lunge for her.

My hands wrap around her throat, and she scratches at my flesh to get me to release her. Lost in my memories, it's not my sister's face I'm seeing, it's not her life I'm watching drain from her eyes as I squeeze.

"Ma-Mama, s-s-stop," she pleads as she thrashes.

I don't know what it is in the moment that makes me stop, but I do. Maybe it's that Giggles' voice isn't, well, *her* voice.

Whatever the reason, I'm grateful because the last people on the planet I want to hurt are my sisters. They're my life, my family. They're everything in a world where I have nothing.

I shove Giggles away from me, and she stumbles but doesn't fall.

"I don't fucking give up," I bark. "I never give up. But I do live in reality, not some fantasy of sunshine and roses."

She shoves her hands in her pockets and rocks back on her heels. "None of us live in a fantasy world, Mama. But some of us need to hold onto hope. I choose to hold on with both hands."

Hope? Hope is foolish. Hope rips your heart out and stomps on it. Hope drags you deeper into the pits of hell faster than evil ever could.

But that's my problem, not hers.

"Fuck," I mutter. "I'm sorry, G. I, uh, lost it there for a minute."

"Ya better find it, Mama," she says as she starts toward the clubhouse. "Find it before it's lost forever."

I watch her walk away, her words flashing in my mind like a neon sign. This isn't the first time I've gone loco on Giggles. She seems to bring out the worst in me. Probably because I see so much of myself in her, and I've never been a fan of looking in mirrors.

Find it before it's lost forever.

It.

My sanity. My give a damn. My heart. My soul. My humanity. Call it what you want, it doesn't matter. *It* is the one thing that separates me from the vile humans we take out.

I used to be a pie-eyed girl who thought the world ran on unicorn farts and glitter. Then I learned that unicorns don't exist, farts stink, and glitter makes a fucking mess. And that's when I started to lose it.

The quiet of the night surrounds me as I begin to clean up

the target area. Memories invade the silence, transporting me to a time and place I'd rather forget.

"Where are you going?"

My big sister, Martina, freezes with her hand on the doorknob and glances over her shoulder at me.

"You're supposed to be in bed, Mari," she snaps.

I lift the glass of water I'm holding. "I was thirsty."

Her eyes dart back and forth between me and the door. "Well, go back to bed."

"But where are you going?" I ask again.

Mommy and Daddy went out again and put her in charge. She was mad because she had a date with her boyfriend, but they told her she'd be grounded if she didn't babysit.

"I've got a date," she whispers, as if we aren't the only two people in the house. "Just go back to bed."

"But I can't be home alone," I remind her. "I'm only ten."

"And you'll be sleeping. Just lock the door behind me. You'll be fine."

Martina is gone before I can argue. I trudge forward and flip the lock before going upstairs to my room. For my sister's sake, I hope she gets home before our parents do, otherwise, they'll kill her.

My cell phone vibrates, snapping me out of my thoughts, and I pull it out of my pocket. I read the text from Harlow, letting us know that she's calling church for nine in the morning. As it's the middle of the night, I decide to stay at the clubhouse rather than ride to my loft in the city.

Twenty minutes later, I'm curled up under the comforter in one of the spare rooms, staring at the ceiling. I know I should sleep, but after days like today, sleep never comes easy. And it always comes with nightmares.

But unlike most people, my nightmares actually happened. I lived through the pain of losing a sister to monsters, of losing my parents to grief. I lived through the worst that the world has to offer.

Find it before it's lost forever.

What if I don't want to find it? What if finding it means losing *myself* forever?

CHAPTER 2

Benson

"HEY, Ben, there's someone I'd like you to meet."

My sister-in-law sits across from me at one of the tables in the school cafeteria, which has become the permanent meeting and organizational space after school lets out every day. I move the flyers I've been working on to the side and rest my elbows on the laminate top. Forcing a smile, I glance at the man who sits next to Jenny.

"Ben, this is Pastor Ron. He heard about Simon's disappearance on the news and wanted to come today to help with the search efforts."

The flask in my pocket seems to burn through the denim, letting me know it's still there, waiting to be tipped to my lips.

I reach across the table to shake the pastor's hand. "Thank you for coming."

"It's my pleasure," he says. "Times like these, a community needs to pull together."

You're a day late and a dollar short, preacher man.

"I appreciate that."

"Pastor Ron, today marks the one-month anniversary of Simon's abduction." Jenny talks as if it's something to be celebrated. "We were hoping you'd say a prayer to kick off the candlelight vigil tonight."

We were hoping? What's this 'we' bullshit?

"I'd be honored," he says. "Is there anything I can do to help before then?"

I pick up a stack of flyers and hand it to him. "If you could go around town and post these, that would be great. The detectives advised us to change the flyers up every once in a while as different photos may spark different leads."

He takes the papers. "Of course." He turns to Jenny. "What time should I be back for the vigil?"

"You do know it's my son that's missing, right?" I bark, annoyed that he's looking to her for information.

Pastor Ron levels his gaze on me for a moment, almost as if he wants to admonish me for being rude. Part of me wants to dare him to try, but mostly I just want him to go away. I want everyone to go away because if they weren't here, it'd mean Simon was.

"You're right," he says with a dip of his chin. "I apologize. I've dealt with the families of missing children several times over the years, and typically I communicate with a spokesperson for the family. I assumed that was Jenny in this case, but clearly I was mistaken."

I heave a sigh. "No, no. You're fine," I insist, guilt settling in. Fuck, I need a drink. "I'm sorry for being rude. It's been a long month, and I'm—"

"Mr. Green, please," Pastor Ron says. "You don't need to apologize to me. I can't imagine what you're going through, and it's understandable that you're a bit on edge."

Pushing up from the bench attached to the cafeteria table, I nod. "The vigil starts at dusk. Thank you for coming today."

Without waiting for a response, I turn and walk out of the large room. I make my way to a set of doors that open up to the playground where Simon would've had recess. Out of sight of everyone, I grab my flask and unscrew the top before downing half of the contents.

The liquor warms a path to my gut, but it doesn't chase away the perpetual darkness that's wrapped itself around me. I don't think there's anything on the planet capable of doing that. Nothing but finding my son.

If I'd have known that I'd never see my son again, I'd have let him skip school that day. Maybe then we'd be home, and I'd be helping him with his homework, not sitting here drinking because I have no idea where he is.

At first, I was hopeful. The cops were, too. But then twenty-four hours passed, then forty-eight. And everyone knows the first forty-eight hours are the most critical. The odds of finding Simon drastically reduced after that. Sure, we might find a body, if we're lucky.

No. No, no, no. He's alive. He has to be.

I swallow down the remaining alcohol before screwing the cap back on the flask and shoving it into my pocket. Making my way to the swings, I sit and push off with my feet, letting a slight breeze cool the sweat beading on my forehead.

"Ah, Katie," I whisper. "I could really use your help finding out little boy."

My dead wife doesn't answer, of course, but talking to her is the only thing that feels normal lately. She and I used to talk about everything and anything. For hours, we'd discuss the future, our hopes and dreams. But never once did we talk about what we'd do if tragedy struck. Maybe we were naive, or maybe we were just stupid. Either way, the situation I find myself in never crossed my mind as a possibility.

"Mr. Green?"

I whip my head around and see a man standing near the posts of the swings. He isn't anyone I recognize, but he's wearing a suit that screams FBI, and fear squeezes my heart with a meaty fist.

Hopping off the swing, I close the distance between us. "You found Simon."

It's a statement, not a question. There's something in the man's expression that makes me sure of my words. He appears... resigned?

"Mr. Green, I'm Special Agent Calhoun." We shake hands before he sweeps his to indicate a picnic table off to the side of the playground. "Why don't we have a seat?"

Shaking my head vigorously, I reply. "No. You can tell me whatever you have to tell me right here."

Agent Calhoun narrows his eyes for a moment, and I can't help but wonder if he's assessing my stability. "Okay. Yes, we found Simon."

Air whooshes past my lips, and my shoulders sag. My knees buckle, and Agent Calhoun grabs me by the arms to keep me on my feet and urges me to the picnic table. Once we're seated, he continues.

"Mr. Green, do you have family inside?" he asks. "Anyone who can sit with you while we talk?"

I scrub my hands over my face. "I, uh... Jenny, my sister-in-law, is in the cafeteria. Her husband, my brother... Uh, Hank should be here soon."

"Maybe we should wait for Hank," he suggests.

"No," I snap. "No. Just tell me whatever it is you came to tell me."

"Well, as you deduced, we found Simon." The agent takes out his cell phone and taps on the screen a few times. "We don't know his precise location, but I can assure you, the cyber-crimes unit is doing everything they can to track him down."

"Cyber-crimes?"

"Yes." Agent Calhoun turns his cell around so I can see the screen, and I immediately wish he wouldn't have. "It seems Simon has been abducted by a trafficking ring that operates all over the east coast."

My eyes blur as I stare at the image of Simon. He's standing on what appears to be a stage and shackles around his ankles keep him from running. There's a spotlight above him, casting him in an eerie glow, and Simon has his hand over his eyes to shield them as one would do against the sun.

The suit he's wearing looks like it cost more than what I used to make in a week. He's alive, but I can't tell if he's hurt in any way. And that shatters me in ways I didn't know were possible.

But the worst part of what I'm staring at isn't my son or the way he's being held. No, it's the countdown clock at the bottom of the screen and the consistently increasing dollar amount next to it.

What the actual fuck?!

Agent Calhoun is right… they found my son. But he's being auctioned off like some collector's item on eBay.

CHAPTER 3

Mama

FIVE MONTHS LATER...

"WE'RE NOT in fucking Kansas anymore, Toto."

I smirk at Spooks, our Sergeant at Arms, who's standing to my right with a gun in one hand and an ax in the other. Harlow and Peppermint, our Prez and VP, are to the left of me, and their expressions are no doubt mirroring my own look of horror. As members of the Devil's Handmaidens MC, we've seen a lot in our efforts to rescue human trafficking victims but what we're staring at has to be the worst.

"What the fuck is this?" Giggles mutters.

We've been tracking this new ring for months, and this is the first time we haven't been too late. Flesh Dealer 2.0, as the leader calls himself, has operated in the shadows and on the dark web, but the tip we received this morning gave us the lead we needed to finally do some good.

"Pep, Spooks, and Giggles, scour the building and find those kids," Harlow barks.

They run to do her bidding while I assess our surroundings.

The room is large and reminds me of a mini movie theater, only more lavish. Burgundy and black velvet cover almost every surface, and the lighting is dim to create an opulent atmosphere.

There are five rows of seating which I wind my way through. Next to each plush chair is a small round table with a keypad inlaid into the top. As I make my way toward the front of the space, I level my gaze on what appears to be a stage with a large drop-down screen.

I hop up onto the stage, careful of my own ax, and my stomach rolls. The wood is blood-stained, and there are four sets of shackles attached to the floor. The screen is blank, but I can only imagine what was playing on it before we stormed the place ten minutes ago.

I've heard of places like this, spaces where sick fucks parade victims around like cattle at a farm auction. They watch them, judge them, and then bid on them like they're merchandise to be purchased. All to satisfy their disgusting fantasies.

"The chick that called in the tip said that business was conducted in the same building where the kids were being held," Harlow says with disdain. "But I wasn't picturing this."

Malachi and Nico have tried to tap into the auctions but have never been successful. As soon as they get close, the site is shut down and the auction canceled. So when we got the tip this morning, we didn't even try to see the auction. We came straight here.

Shaking my head, I bend down and lift one of the shackles. The chain rattles, the sound sending a tingling sensation down my spine, and not the good kind.

"Motherfucker," I mumble. "Har, I thought the Ricci family was bad. Malachi's father had nothing on Flesh Dealer 2.0."

"No shit." She pulls out her cell phone and sends a text before pocketing the device. "Let's get those kids and get the hell outta here. This place is making my skin crawl."

"You and me both, Prez."

Just as we reach the door, gunfire erupts, and we pick up our pace. There's no time to get lost in our heads about what kind of person even steps foot in a place like this. We can do that later, after the victims are safe back at Devil's Double Down, the club-owned casino.

As I run, I jump over the bodies of guards and Armani-wearing pricks we've already taken out. I don't give them a second thought as Harlow and I join the other three in their fight to rescue the *merchandise*.

When the last man is eliminated, the five of us take a minute to catch our breath. I glance down and grimace at the blood coating my jeans. Axes and knives are great weapons, but they wreak havoc on my wardrobe.

"Uh, Prez, you might want to call for reinforcements."

I turn to look at what Peppermint is seeing and rage boils in my gut. This space is a far cry from the upscale theater room. The floor is concrete and dirty, and the walls are the same. The entire area is cold and depressing. And the worst thing is the metal cages lining the walls, each one occupied by a person. Some are caked in dirt and wearing raggedy clothing while others are clean and sporting dresses or suits that are far too old for them.

Children. They're filled with fucking children.

"Malachi is on his way with Gill and two more vans," Harlow says, her tone low and menacing. "I'm gonna go outside to meet them when they get here." She turns on her heel and disappears out of the dingy space.

While Giggles and Spooks start working to unlock the cages with a key I assume they got off one of the guard's bodies, I stand frozen. I've been a Devil's Handmaiden for years now and this is the worst captivity setup I've ever seen. If the dirt and cages weren't enough to make a person vomit, the smell would be.

Peppermint and I go behind them to help the scared,

crying children out. I'm dimly aware of Pep whispering reassurances, but it's hard to hear her over the blood rushing through my system and the thunderous pound of my heart.

"Who are you?"

I smile at the girl I'm assisting, who can't be more than twelve. "My name is Marisol, but you can call me Mama."

She scrunches up her nose causing the dried dirt on her face to crack. "I already have a mom." Tears fill her eyes. "I miss my mom."

"Aw, sweetie, I know," I assure her. "We're going to get you back to her as quickly as we can, okay?" She nods. "What's your name?"

"Tammy."

"Well, Tammy, if you'd feel better calling me Marisol or Mari, you can. Mama is just a nickname."

Please don't call me Mari.

Tammy tilts her head slightly as if considering her options and then shrugs. "Mama is fine. As long as it's just a nickname, and you're not trying to take my mom's place." She lowers her head and fidgets with her hands. "The bad men told me I was getting a new mommy. I don't want a new one."

"Then you're in luck, Tammy, because we're going to get you home to your mom." I grab her hand and guide her toward the huddle of other kids by the door. "Can you hang tight here for a few minutes while I help get the rest freed? Can you do that for me?"

Tammy nods, and I move to another open cage, then another and another. It feels like hours tick by before I reach the last one, but I know it's only a few minutes. When I squat in front of it, my heart skips a beat at the hope shining in the little boy's eyes.

How the fuck is anyone hopeful after being held in this place?

"Hey, kiddo," I say as softly as my fury will allow and reach my hand inside to take his. He backs away from me, the faint light in his eyes dimming, and my heart sinks. "It's okay," I croon. "Can you come out for me?"

He shakes his head, and his shaggy dark brown hair falls over his forehead. He swipes it away, and it's then that I notice a silicone band on his wrist. I narrow my eyes to read the embossed writing on the red bracelet. Four letters are all it takes to tell me the kind of horror this kid has been put through.

SOLD.

Motherfucking sold.

"Son of a bitch," I mutter, and he cowers further into the corner. "Oh, kiddo, I'm sorry." Heaving a sigh, I drop to my ass and cross my legs Indian style. "I'm not mad at you, little man. Never at you."

He stares at me for a long moment, but when he opens his mouth to speak, Harlow steps up next to me, and he slams his mouth shut.

"Mama, we need to get outta here," she demands. "We have no idea if anyone else will be showing up, and I want to be long gone if they do."

"Working on it, Prez," I say. "Go ahead and get the others loaded up. Little man and I will be out in a minute."

Harlow hesitates, but then she spins on her heel and walks away. I'm aware of the shuffle of feet as she and my sisters get the other children out of the building, but I never take my eyes off the little boy.

"What's your name?" I ask him.

He shrugs.

"How old are you?"

Again, the boy shrugs.

"Mama, let's go!"

Harlow's shout seems to echo off the concrete around me. I watch the kid, and his entire body begins to shake. I know he's scared, but we aren't the bad guys.

And we're out of time.

Hating myself for it, I shift to my knees and lean my upper body into the cage and grab him by the arms to drag him out. He kicks at me, and I take a small foot to the face. Pain radiates through my cheek, but I ignore it. I need to get him out and whatever happens to me in the process doesn't matter.

"I'm so sorry, little man," I say, trying to remain soothing to him.

"No, no, no." He repeats the word over and over again, screaming it as loud as he can.

"I'm not gonna hurt you, I promise." When we clear the cage, I wrap my arms around his torso and lift him as I stand. "You're safe now. You're safe."

I race toward the exit with him thrashing against me. He continues to shout 'no', and I keep reassuring him as best I can. When I burst through the door, I suck in a deep breath of fresh air.

Malachi is standing at the back of one of the vans, a syringe in his hand. I know it contains a sedative, something we always have ready, just in case, but I shake my head at him.

"No. He's fine."

"Mama, c'mon," Malachi cajoles. "You can barely hold onto him."

"He's fine," I snap. "We're fine."

"No, no, no," the boy repeats like a mantra.

When Harlow pulls up next to the van on her Harley, the boy calms. I still as his head turns to look at the bike.

"Daddy?" he mumbles.

"Daddy?" I say. "Does your dad ride a motorcycle?"

He nods.

"Oh." Well, shit. This might not be so hard to get him back to the casino after all. "Would you like to ride on my motorcycle?"

Again, he nods.

"Okay, then. You're in luck. I've got my bike just over there." I nod toward my Harley, its custom paint job gleaming in the moonlight. "We can ride it, but I'm going to need you to be very still and hold on tight. Can you do that for me?"

"Y-yes," he croaks.

Malachi and Harlow exchange a look, but I don't give it a second thought. I carry him to the bike and help him get situated on the seat.

"Before we go, can you tell me your name?"

He lowers his head, much like Tammy did, and fidgets with his hands. "They called me Ninety-Seven."

A number. All those sick fucks gave these kids were numbers.

"And what did your parents call you? What's your real name?"

He swallows before lifting his head up and staring me in the eyes.

"Simon. My name is Simon."

CHAPTER 4

Benson

"I'M SORRY, MR. GREEN."

I throw my cell at the wall, and it shatters. That's the fourth phone I've broken in the last six months, and the millionth time Agent Calhoun has apologized for not having any new information on my son. When he showed me that video of Simon being auctioned off, I never dreamed another five months would pass by without finding him.

Oh, there have been more videos, more auctions, but they all end the same: with the auction being cut short, and Simon disappearing into the ether again.

If life was a shitshow before, it's a dumpster fire on steroids now. Losing Katie was bad enough, but I had Simon. We had each other. And now I have no one.

You've got Jack and Jim.

Jack Daniels, Jim Beam, and Jose Cuervo are the only things I can count on and even that is dependent on the day. Some are worse than others and no amount of liquor will chase the demons away.

"Where the hell are you, Simon?" I mumble to the empty house.

My mind wanders as I stride toward the kitchen to grab a beer.

"What the fuck do you mean he's not here?"

"Simon Green was picked up by his father," the receptionist *informs me for the second time.*

I slap my hands on the counter and lean toward her. "I'm his father!" I shout, garnering the attention of teachers and staff making their way through the halls.

The clink of the bottle cap as I toss it into the sink jolts me into another memory.

"Benson Green, father of Simon Gr — "

"Don't say it," I snarl. My head pounds a steady beat against my temples. "As long as you aren't doing jack to find my son, you don't get to say his name."

The cop shakes his head. "How the hell am I supposed to find Simon when I spend so much time picking you up for drunk and disorderlies?" He locks eyes with me and sighs. "Look, Ben, you know we're doing everything we can to locate Simon. And the FBI is using all of their resources to try and ascertain where the auctions are being held. But Phi — "

"Philly is a big city," I finish for him. "Yeah, you keep saying that. And I still don't give a shit." Bile climbs up my throat. "It's been three months, man. Three months he's been missing, three months of attempts to sell my son, and you're no closer to finding him than you were on day one."

I lift the beer bottle to my lips and groan when nothing comes out. Twelve ounces of booze doesn't last nearly as long as it used to. After chucking it into the trash, I open the fridge to grab another. As I twist the cap off the bottle, pounding starts on the front door.

"Coming," I shout before taking a long pull from the Bud Light. The knocking becomes louder, more insistent, and I roll my eyes. "Jesus, I'm fucking coming," I mutter under my breath.

As I yank open the door, I gulp some more brew. There's

only one person who knocks like this, and I'm gonna need all the fortification I can get to deal with him.

"Shit, Benny." Hank, my older brother, pushes past me with a shake of his head. "I've been trying to call you all morning." He scans the room, and his gaze lands on the broken cell phone. "At least now I know you weren't ignoring me."

"What do you want Hank?"

I slam the door and stalk to the couch where I flop down.

"You were supposed to work today," he reminds me. "But I see you forgot."

"Didn't forget," I tell him with a shrug. "Just don't care."

Hank throws his arms up. "What are you gonna do when Simon comes back, huh?" he demands. "You can't hold down a job, you don't show up when I give you work so you can earn money to keep this roof over your head. Katie's life insurance isn't going to last forever, ya know?"

Why the hell does he think I drink?

"I'm very aware of my financial situation," I snap and jump to my feet. "But some things are more important than money."

"And everything is more important than alcohol," he counters. "Fuck, Benny. I know you're struggling. I can't imagine how hard this is for you. But drinking yourself to death isn't the answer."

I stalk toward my brother and get within inches of his face. "That's right, big brother," I begin. "You can't imagine. You go home every night to Jenny and the kids. You get to eat dinner with them, talk to them about your day, tuck them in at night. Your perfect life is fully intact. And until it's not, don't come in here and judge me and my choices."

He stares at me for a long moment, so long I start to think he's going to back down, but then he opens his mouth. "You're not the only one who lost Katie and Simon. We all loved them, too."

My shoulders tense. "Loved? Loved?" I repeat. "One minute you're berating me for what Simon will be coming home to and the next you're talking about him as if he's dead and gone forever. Which is it, Hank? Because it can't be both!"

"You know what I meant. I don't think Simon is dead, Benny. I don't."

He wraps his hand around the back of my neck and hauls me to his chest. I push against him, but he doesn't let up. He never lets up. All of my anger dissipates in an instant, replaced by overwhelming anguish, and I let my older brother, my life-long protector, hold me up under the weight of it.

I know I don't deserve the comfort he's offering, the support he's giving me. I stopped being deserving of it months ago when the cops thought maybe he had something to do with Simon's disappearance, and I believed them. At the time, it was the only thing that made sense. Who else would Simon get into a car with?

But Hank didn't have anything to do with it. Of course, he didn't. He's my brother, Simon's uncle. He values family as much as I do. Hank is a good man, and when I think about the way I treated him, I'm ashamed.

"Simon is going to come home, Benny. They'll find him."

I wish I believed that.

The problem with his words is they don't sound true. All I hear is false assurances that someone says when they're afraid to spit out what they're really thinking.

"And in the meantime, you need to get yourself together. Simon is going to need you when he comes home. He's going to need you more than ever."

I nod as I straighten away from Hank.

"Good." He slaps me on the back. "I have to get back to work. Do you need anything before I go?"

"Nah." I take a deep breath as I swipe the wetness from

my cheeks. "I need to go get a new phone and then…" I shrug. "I don't know what."

"Why don't you come over for dinner? We'd love to have you, and I know your niece and nephew would enjoy seeing you."

Vigorously, I shake my head. That's too much. I can't be around them, not yet. "Maybe another time."

"Right." Hank's shoulders slump, and I know I'm hurting him. But I can't help it. Being around kids isn't something I can handle. Not when my own is still out there somewhere. "Well, call me if you need anything."

"I will," I assure him. "Go, get back to work. I'm fine."

"You're not, but I'm going." He strides to the door and yanks it open. Before he leaves, he looks over his shoulder. "Love you, Benny."

"You too."

After he's gone, I stare at the closed door for several long minutes. I said I was going to go and get a new phone, and I need to. If Simon is found, I need to be reachable. But leaving the house, going to the store, interacting with people… it's all just too much.

Turning on my heel, I stalk to the kitchen and snag the half-full bottle of Jim Beam from the counter. I don't bother with a glass or ice before making my way to Simon's bedroom.

I spend the rest of the day curled up on the twin mattress, lost in my head and drowning my sorrows with as much booze as my body can handle.

CHAPTER 5
Mama

"DID YOU HEAR FROM HIM TODAY?"

I glance at Giggles as I stride into her kitchen, where she's feeding Simon and Noah a snack. It's been a week since we rescued Simon and the others, and he's the only one who hasn't been picked up by a parent or family member.

"No, little man, I didn't," I reply as I ruffle his hair. Simon's face falls, so I tilt my mouth into a smile. "But hey, that just means you get to hang out with Noah a bit longer."

Giggles and I exchange a look, and I shrug. I'm the only person Simon has opened up to since his rescue, but I worry that he'll lose faith in me if we don't get him home soon.

"Harlow's called church," I tell her. "We need to be at the clubhouse in an hour."

"Okay, boys," she begins. "Finish up so we can head out."

"Are we taking your bike?" Simon asks me.

"We can, if that's what you want."

He nods as he shoves his last cookie into his mouth. After he swallows, he grins. "I'm ready."

Riding my Harley seems to be the one thing that takes Simon's mind off of everything else going on, and if that's what it takes to make him happy, so be it. It's not as if riding is a hardship for me.

An hour later, Simon and Noah are sitting in front of the television watching a movie, and the club officers are situated around the table in the meeting room.

"I can't come to the phone right now, but if—"

Disconnecting the call, I groan with frustration. I've lost track of how many times I've called the phone number we found for Benson Green and not gotten an answer. If my calls were under normal circumstances, I'd get it. He doesn't recognize my number so he's not answering. But his fucking son is missing so every call is important, unknown number or not.

"What kind of father doesn't answer the damn phone when his son is missing?" Spooks demands from across the table. "We've been calling for a fucking week and based on the police reports, Simon was abducted six months ago."

I turn toward Harlow and frown. "I know protocol is to have family come to us, but I don't think that's going to happen in Simon's case."

Harlow nods but says nothing.

"Nico did find an address for Benson," Peppermint says. "I think it's time to vote on whether or not to use it."

"I'm not crazy about sending any of you to a man's home who has a slew of arrests and a very apparent drinking problem," Harlow says.

"Aw, Prez," Giggles sing-songs. "You worried about us?"

Harlow scowls. "Always." When several of us open our mouths to protest, she holds up a hand. "Don't. I know you can all handle yourselves. Hell, you can handle pretty much any fucking thing that's thrown at you. But we're talking about a parent who's trapped in some sort of internal hell, and that's probably more dangerous than the traffickers we deal with on a regular basis."

"Dangerous or not, we have to try," I say. "Unless we go to the cops or call child services."

"No," Harlow barks. "You saw those police reports. As soon as the FBI stepped in, Philly PD practically closed the case. They didn't do anything when Simon was missing so they don't deserve any of the glory now that he's safe." She takes a deep breath. "And the FBI cyber-crimes division is a joke. They never even realized Nico was poking around and the reason the auctions were always shut down." She shakes her head. "No, we handle this in-house. Besides, Flesh Dealer 2.0 is good. Too good. I don't trust for a second that law enforcement isn't in his pocket."

"Understood," I agree. "And I don't want to call child services, but Simon can't stay here."

"I hate to point out the flaw in taking Simon home," Tahiti, our former SAA, says.

"Then don't."

"But I will," she says. "Taking Simon home comes with more complications than just a depressed dad," Tahiti finishes. "We still haven't determined if Benson had anything to do with Simon's disappearance. It doesn't look like it on the surface but looks can be deceiving."

"He did lose his wife not long before Simon's abduction," Story adds. "I hacked into his former employer's database, and he was fired not long after that. Drinking on the job... when he showed up. And the slew of arrests he's racked up since Simon went missing points to a man who's slightly off his rocker."

"Can you blame him?" I counter hotly.

"I'm not saying he didn't have reason to lose his shit," Story explains. "But that can also lead to bad decisions."

"Like orchestrating your own child's disappearance? Is that what you really think, that he had something to do with it?"

"Look, none of us know what really happened," Harlow

points out. "And that's the problem. It's not like Simon is giving us much help."

"He's seven!" I shout as I shoot to my feet and begin to pace the room. "And he went through hell. Of course, he's not much help."

"Mama, what the fuck is going on with you?" Peppermint asks from her seat. "You're normally a steel vault with your emotions, but not with this case. Why?"

"Because they're kids."

"We've rescued kids before. Lots of 'em."

I stop in my tracks and glare at my VP. "Does it matter? Shouldn't we all be pissed the fuck off about this?"

"We are," Spooks says quietly, which is odd for her. "Every single case pisses us off. But we deal with it. We have to."

"And I'm dealing with it," I snap.

No, you're not. Not well, at least.

Harlow stands and walks toward me. When she's within arm's reach, she rests her hands on my shoulders. "Does this have anything to do with your sister?"

She might as well have slugged me in the stomach with a sledgehammer. I don't talk about Martina. Hell, I try not to think about her. But lately, with Flesh Dealer 2.0, she's constantly in my head.

Taking a deep breath, I shrug out of Harlow's hold and square my shoulders. "This isn't personal. I just want to reunite a little boy with his father. I don't know why you're all making that out to be a bad thing."

With that, I storm out of church. I've no doubt I'll pay for it later, but at the moment, I don't give a shit. The air in the room was suffocating me. Their questions, their concern... it was becoming debilitating.

Does this have anything to do with your sister?

Of course, it fucking does. It shouldn't, but it does. When Martina went missing, my parents did everything that Benson

Green has done. They organized search parties, candlelight vigils, and press conferences. They worked with the police and the FBI when it became clear that she'd been transported across state lines.

They did everything they were told to do, and it still didn't matter. Martina was lost forever. Mom and Dad turned to alcohol, and when that wasn't enough, they started using heroin. That lasted several years, and then they were gone too.

"Mama, c'mon back in."

I swipe at the tears I hadn't even realized were streaming down my cheeks and turn to face Harlow. She's standing with her hand on the door to the meeting room, her eyes blazing with understanding. She knows my history. Every ugly detail. Shit, she was there when the worst of it happened, a few years after I buried my parents. And she's never brought it up... until today.

"I don't want to talk about Martina," I say, remaining in place.

"And we won't," she assures me. "Not until you're ready. But, Mama, all those women in there, they love you. They deserve to know why you're so caught up in this one."

"I could be wrong."

Harlow tilts her head. "Do you really believe that?"

"I don't know, Har. I just..." I shrug. "I don't know."

"C'mon, we've got a vote pending and need you," she says, letting my uncertainty hang in the air between us. "Let's get through church and then you and I are going to talk."

"Okay."

I follow her back into the room and flinch when the door slams behind me. Fucking hell, I'm an enforcer. Why am I so jumpy?

Ghosts tend to have that effect on people.

"Now that we're all here, we need to vote on whether or

not we take Simon home or continue to try and reach his dad," Harlow says.

"I think that's pretty obvious," Spooks chimes in. "Unless Mama wants to adopt the kid, he needs to go home."

There's a teasing quality to her tone, and I huff out a laugh in an attempt at normalcy. If I don't laugh about it, I'd cry. And I can't afford to cry. Not anymore.

"And can we ensure his safety if we do that?" Giggles asks. "We've talked about the potential problems, all the unknowns with Benson. Not to mention, we still don't know who Flesh Dealer 2.0 is," she adds. "We haven't determined if he was one of the men we killed during the rescue, but my gut tells me he wasn't."

Oh, Flesh Dealer 2.0 is still out there. The fuck isn't stupid enough to actually be present at one of the auctions.

"All those in favor of taking Simon home, say 'aye'," Harlow instructs. When we all say 'aye', she nods. "Good. Now, we just need to figure out who will take him."

"I'll do it," I say without thinking. All eyes turn to me, and I lift one shoulder. "What? Simon trusts me. And I can keep him safe."

Harlow narrows her eyes. "Are you sure?"

I know why she's asking. I even appreciate her concern. But this is something I have to do. It's something *only* I can do.

"I'm sure."

CHAPTER 6
Benson

"MR. BENSON, my name is Marisol, and I'd appreciate it if you'd return my call. It's regarding your son, Simon."

I delete the voicemail before listening to the rest. They're all the same. This Marisol bitch wants to talk to me about Simon, and it's very important that I call her back.

No fucking thank you.

I've been fielding calls from reporters for months, and I'm over it. Hell, even a representative from Dateline contacted me. Apparently, an abducted boy who shows up on dark web human trafficking auction sites is good entertainment.

But it's not entertainment. It's my life, my son's life. It's real, and I have zero interest in helping some two-bit news chaser get the 'story of a lifetime'.

There are four more voicemails from the same number, and I delete those before shoving my cell in my pocket and straddling my motorcycle. Without Simon, I don't ride as often as I used to, but it's the one thing that makes me feel alive in a world where all I want to do is die.

Maybe I'll get lucky and lay the bike down one of these days.

Backing out of the garage, I chastise myself for the thought. Simon is out there, and my death won't do him any good. Sure, Hank and Jenny would take him in, and they'd give him a damn good life. But he's already lost a mother. I can't let him lose a father too.

Wind whips through my hair as I travel through the residential neighborhoods, putting distance between me and… everything. The vibrations of my bike rumble through me, calming me in a way that shouldn't be possible.

I ride for hours, no clear destination other than away. Miles and miles separate me from my reality, but I still can't escape it. Not completely.

When I head back home, I make sure to take a route that passes a liquor store, knowing I drank the last of my stash earlier in the day. By the time I get to the house, three bottles of booze in my saddlebags, the sun has fallen beneath the horizon. I pull into the garage and kill the engine, but I sit there for a minute, dreading going into the empty house.

I glance around the garage, staring at all the tools I've accumulated over the years. Back before Katie got sick, I loved tinkering and building things. Yes, it's what I did for work, but it didn't stop there. I'd even built the arch Katie and I stood under at our wedding.

Pain licks my insides as I think about that arch. It's long gone now, burned into ash after her funeral. It had stood in our backyard as a sort of entrance to where her flower beds were located, but I couldn't bear to look at it after she was gone. So I chopped it down and set it on fire.

"Daddy, what are you doing?"

"Go back inside, kiddo," I snap, staring into the orange flames.

"But that was Mommy's special door," he cries as he latches onto my hand and tugs. "Daddy, how is Mommy going to get to her fairies without her special door?"

Simon's words stab me through the heart, piercing through the scarred tissue and ripping open the wound. Katie loved telling our son stories about how walking through the arch could transport a person to a special, magical world full of fairies and all things happy.

But Katie is gone, and it's time he learns that there's nothing magical in the world.

What I wouldn't give to go back in time, to make sure that Katie's stories hadn't died with her. But they did.

As I swing my leg over the seat to stand, my phone rings. I pull it out of my pocket and groan when I see the number flashing on the screen.

"Ignore," I mumble as I stab the red icon to silence the call. "Take a fucking hint, Marisol whatever the hell your last name is."

A minute later, my phone dings with a notification, no doubt a voicemail from her demanding that I call her back. I don't bother checking the device as I grab the Jack, Jim, and Jose out of my saddlebags and carry the alcohol inside.

I shouldn't mix the three, but as I stood in the liquor store trying to make up my mind about which friend to invite home, I heard the newscast on the stupid television that the guy behind the counter is always watching. I don't know if you're aware, but a lot of newscasts start with the date. And this one was no different.

When it dawned on me what today is, I said 'fuck it' and decided to have a real party. All three of my friends came home with me, and all three are gonna take me on a wild ride into oblivion.

I open the bottle of Jack Daniels first and swallow several large gulps as I traipse to the living room and flop down onto the couch. How did I not realize what today is?

Because your mind's been a little preoccupied.

That's no excuse to forget my son's birthday.

Fuck, fuck, fuck.

Lifting the bottle, I tip it to my lips and when there's a knock on my door, I almost choke on the mouthful of whiskey. It's almost eleven, too late for visitors, so who the fuck is interrupting my pity party?

I ignore whoever it is and take another swig, but the intruder doesn't take a hint and continues to knock. After getting to my feet, I stride to the door and yank it open.

And promptly swallow my tongue.

"Mr. Green? Benson Green?"

"I, uh…"

The woman with dark curly hair looks over her shoulder toward the vehicle idling in my driveway before facing me again.

"I've been trying to get a hold of you," she says.

Her voice sounds familiar, but I can't quite place it. I rack my brain, and she speaks again.

"I left several messages about Simon."

Recognition hits me like a freight train, and my anger spikes. "Man, you people will do anything for a story, won't you?"

She arches a perfect brow and crosses her arms over her chest. My gaze lowers, taking in the way her tits pillow above the deep V-neck of her black top. I'd love to blame my staring on the alcohol, but I'm not that deep into the bottle yet.

"Excuse me," she snarks. "You people?"

I lift my head and force my eyes to focus on her face. Her stupid, beautiful, angry face. "Reporters," I bark, raising the bottle in my hand. "Here's a story for you, Miss Marisol. My wife died after a long battle with cancer, my son was abducted from what should've been a very safe place, and I don't know if I'll ever see him again. So here I am, on what should be a happy day, drinking myself silly to forget all the shit I've been through."

"You didn't even listen to my full voicemails, did you?"

"If you're waiting for an apology, you might wanna take a seat because you'll be waiting a long damn time."

Marisol starts to tap her booted foot, and the sound grates on my nerves. "I'm not a reporter, Mr. Green."

"Your point?"

"My point, Mr. Green, is that I've been calling to tell you that we fo—"

"Mama, I gotta pee."

"Seriously?" I scoff. "You've got a kid in the car? What kind of mother brings her child to a strange man's house this late at night?"

"I'm not a mother," she deadpans. "But I am the woman who's bringing a little boy to his father's house." She glares at the liquor bottle in my hand. "Although I'm starting to rethink that decision."

"Lady, I'm in no mood to de—" I press my lips together as her words sink in. "Wait… what did you just say?"

The vehicle lights up from the inside as a door is opened, and it goes out when it's slammed shut. A small flurry of movement has my full attention as a child races from the driveway and up the porch steps, stopping next to Marisol.

"Mama, I really gotta go."

No fucking way. It can't be.

I drop to my knees, unable to remain upright a second longer.

"Simon?"

CHAPTER 7
Mama

"SIMON?"

The little boy standing next to me and tugging on my hand stills as he turns to face his father.

"Daddy?"

Benson looks from Simon to me and back again. The confusion on his face is understandable, but entirely his fault. He'd have known his son was in the car if he'd bothered to listen to my voicemails or let me explain who I am and why I'm here.

"Hey, Simon, why don't you run inside and use the bathroom, so you don't pee your pants?" I suggest when Benson remains stunned silent.

Simon nods, but before he can run past his dad, Benson snakes his arm around his son's waist and hauls him to his chest. Simon squirms in only the way kids who are close to peeing their pants do, but he doesn't pull away or resist the hug.

So, this is what a reunion should look like?

After a minute, Simon wiggles out of his dad's hold. "I really gotta pee, Dad."

Benson nods. "Okay."

Simon darts inside, disappearing as he rounds the corner, presumably to the bathroom. Benson stands and glares at me.

"Why the fuck wouldn't you tell me you had my son?"

I smirk. "I did, in my voicemails. Which you clearly didn't bother to listen to completely."

For a split-second, his face softens, and he appears apologetic, but the rage quickly reappears. "Who the hell are you? Why do you have my son?" He steps toward me, getting in my face. "And what the fuck is he calling you Mama?"

A toilet flushes from inside, and Simon comes barreling around the corner, skidding to a stop behind his dad.

"Are you coming inside?" he asks.

"I'll be right there, Simon," his dad responds, keeping his gaze on me. "As soon as she leaves."

Simon rushes forward and grabs my hand before tipping his head back to look at me. "You said you wouldn't leave me, Mama. You said you'd—"

"She's not your mama," Benson snaps.

Simon cowers at the outburst, and I wrap an arm around his shoulder.

"I'm not leaving," I tell the boy as my eyes remain locked on Benson, who practically growls at my words. "At least not tonight."

"I don't think so," Benson snarls.

I drop my stare to the bottle in his hand for a moment and sigh. When I look at the man again, he averts his eyes.

"Look, you've got two options," I start. "The first option, and my personal recommendation, is that I stay because your son, who's been traumatized enough, wants me to stay."

"And the second option?"

"I leave, and Simon goes with me." I shrug. "I guess that would mean you could keep drinking, which... yay for you. But then Simon's trauma worsens, and he starts to wonder why his dad doesn't want—"

"Fine," he pushes out. "You can stay. But just for the night."

I grin, and he scowls. "Good choice." I urge Simon toward his dad. "Be right back."

I turn and rush to the car to grab my bag. Not only did I shove a change of clothes into it, but I also tossed an ax, gun, and knife in before we left the clubhouse. I've got a knife in my boot, as well. One can never be too prepared.

Before returning to the house, I take a minute to call Harlow. She answers on the second ring.

"How'd the family reunion go?" she asks.

"Okay, so far. I didn't tell Simon where we were going, ya know, just in case I got bad juju from Benson. But so far, I don't get the feeling he was involved," I explain. "The man's a drunk, but he loves his son."

"What do you mean he's a drunk?"

"Just that. He so much as opens his mouth and the stench of alcohol smacks ya in the face. I'm gonna stay tonight to make sure he sobers up."

"Mama, you got the boy home. That's the extent of your job."

I bristle. "No, it's not. My job is to make sure he's safe. Until he has a clear-headed parent to take care of him, I can't be sure he is." Taking a deep breath, I hold it in until I'm almost dizzy from it. After blowing out air, I say, "Besides, Simon's buyer is sti—" I press my lips together as the unmistakable sound of a door slamming reaches me. "Shit."

"What?"

"Pretty sure I just got locked out of the house."

Harlow laughs. "Seriously?"

I walk around the corner to face the porch and sure enough, the front door is shut, and the porch light is off.

"Yep," I confirm before striding back to the car. "Dammit. I can't remember the last time I had to pick a lock."

"It's like riding a bike. You'll figure it out."

"I know I will," I snap. "But I shouldn't have to. I just brought the man's son back for fuck's sake."

"Have you had a chance to talk to him, explain where Simon's been?"

I sigh. "No. And honestly, I'm not sure how much to tell him," I admit. "I mean, he has a right to know what happened to Simon, but the rest of it? I don't fucking know, Prez."

"Look, give him the information he needs to know as Simon's father, the details that will help him deal with the trauma his son experienced," she instructs. "As for the rest... tell him what you're comfortable telling him."

"Yeah, okay. I should go."

"Right." Harlow inhales deeply. "Mama, I'm sorry this is happening. I'd handle it all myself if I could."

"No, no, it's okay," I say, and I mean it. It's not her fault this particular trafficker is active again. And it's definitely not her fault I'm the only Devil's Handmaiden who has experience with Flesh Dealer. "I have to handle it. I have to end it."

"I know. And just like a lot of things, I don't have to like it," she says. "We're here if you need anything, you know that, right?"

"Yeah."

"Good. Get inside and deal with things there. And gimme a call tomorrow. We'll take this one day at a time."

"Got it. And Harlow?"

"Yeah?"

"Thank you. I don't know if I've ever told you that before but... thank you."

"No thanks necessary. You're family, Mama. And I'd do anything for family."

With that, she disconnects the call, and I'm left standing in the driveway feeling... Fuck, I don't know what I'm feeling.

Sad?

A little.

Annoyed?

Oh yeah.

Scared?

Out of my damn mind.

Maybe that isn't exactly par for the course for an MC enforcer, but it's reality.

I'm scared because I know what's coming. Simon might feel safe, and Benson will likely think the threat is over. But it's not. And it won't be.

Unless I end it.

CHAPTER 8
Benson

"WHAT DO you mean 'he's back'?"

I pace the length of the living room while Simon sits on the couch, silently watching me with weary eyes.

"Exactly that, Hank," I snap, and when my son burrows deeper into the cushions, I regret my tone. "Some chick showed up on my doorstep, with Simon in tow."

"Some chick?" my brother repeats. "Benny, how much have you had to drink?"

I glance at the almost empty bottle of Jack Daniels that I set on the counter. After slamming the door and locking it, I downed most of the whiskey. With Simon here, it wasn't a smart move, but I needed it. Hell, I need more.

"I've had one drink," I lie. "But that's irrelevant. Simon is home."

"Benny, none of this makes sense," Hank says. "I'm coming over."

"No, you don—"

Hank disconnects the call, and I instantly regret calling him. In my defense, he's my big brother, and I was excited. I *am* excited. My son is home.

"Daddy, are you gonna let Mama in?"

"No," I reply without thinking.

"But you said she could stay."

I whirl around and stalk toward the couch. When I'm in front of it, I crouch down. "Simon, I don't know this woman. For all I know, she's who took you."

My son shakes his head, and tears fill his eyes. "I want her to stay."

My head swims with confusion. Why does he seem so attached to this woman? Why is he acting like he's afraid of me? I don't understand.

I rise to my full height. "Simon, let's get you to bed. We can talk in the morning."

He jumps up off the couch and races toward the door. "No. I'm not tired."

When Simon opens the door, Marisol is bent over with small tools in her hands, but she raises her head quickly.

"Thanks, little man," she says as she straightens and ruffles his hair. She steps inside as if she owns the place, then shuts and locks the door behind her. When she faces Simon again, she crouches in front of him much like I did. "I hate to break it to you, but it's late. I think you should listen to your dad and go to bed."

"But I'm not tired, Mama," he insists even as he yawns.

Grinding my teeth, I hold back the fury at his continuing to call her Mama.

She grabs his hands and grins. "Well, I'm exhausted, and you know the rule."

Simon sighs dramatically. "If the adults go to bed, so do the kids."

"Yep, you got it. So," she begins as she stands and links her fingers with his. "Whaddya say? Wanna show me your room?"

Simon glances at me as if seeking permission, and not sure what else to do, I nod. "Go ahead."

The two of them disappear down the hall while I remain rooted in place.

What. The. Hell?

Their voices carry through the house, Simon's excited and Marisol's patient. Forcing myself out of my stupor, I walk toward the bedroom and lean against the doorframe. My son is sitting on his mattress, already changed into pajamas, and he's animatedly talking about all the toys he can't wait to play with. And Marisol is sitting on the edge of the bed trying to guide him under the covers.

"Oh, and I have tons of superhero action figures." Simon tilts his head. "Hey, you're kinda like a superhero. You saved me from the bad men and brought me home."

My heart squeezes at what I'm sure is an oversimplification.

God, I need a fucking drink.

"I'm not a superhero, little man," she says with a chuckle.

"But Noah said Giggles is his superhero," he insists. "And you and Giggles are sisters, right? So you're a superhero too."

Giggles?

"And Harlow is the head superhero," Simon continues. "That's what Noah said."

So. Many. Questions.

"Noah said a whole lot, didn't he?" she teases, and he nods. "Well, if I'm a superhero, my power is making little boys settle down so they can sleep."

"Aw, that's no fun," he whines.

She stands. "I know. But them's the rules, kid. I'm going to bed, and so is your dad. And when adults go to bed, kids—"

"Kids go to bed," he says, repeating her *rule* from earlier.

Marisol tucks him in and turns to face me. "Your turn."

The urge to bodily throw her out of my house is strong, but I resist. I have no clue what Simon has been through and for whatever reason, he trusts her. Something tells me that him witnessing her murder would not be good for his psyche.

I push off the doorframe and stride toward my son's bed, all the while holding my breath. With the way the night is going, it wouldn't surprise me in the least if he shied away from me. But he doesn't.

Leaning down, I press a kiss to his forehead. "G'night, kiddo. I love you."

"Night, Dad," he mumbles.

I heave a sigh and walk back toward the door. Marisol is standing there, watching, waiting. When I lift my hand to turn the light off, she grabs it and shakes her head.

"He's not good with the dark yet," she whispers.

I narrow my eyes, venom sitting on the tip of my tongue. Rather than spew it, I swallow it down and nod.

Fucking hell.

She turns on her heel and strides down the hall to the living room. Like a damn puppy, I follow. What else is there to do?

Just as I open my mouth to start asking the millions of questions swirling in my brain, the sound of a key in the locked front door cuts through the silence.

Marisol's eyes dart to me. "Are you expecting someone?" She bends down to reach in her boot and stands with a knife in her hand. "Answer me, Benson," she whisper yells.

"What the..." I move to open the door, remembering that Hank said he was coming over. "Get in here," I demand as I grab his coat sleeve and yank him inside. Once the door is closed again, I turn to her. "It's my brother."

Her shoulders slump. "Oh."

"What the hell were you gonna do with that?" Hank asks as he stares at the knife she's still holding.

She shrugs. "Whatever I had to."

"You would've stabbed him?" I ask incredulously.

She smirks as, again, she shrugs. "What? My gun is in my bag. Stabbing was the only option."

Stunned stupid, I stare at her. "I... You..." I shake my head. "I need a drink."

Hank groans, but I ignore him as I head for the bottle of Jim Beam I bought earlier. I reach for it, but it's snatched from the counter before I can get my fingers around the neck. Slowly, I turn and see Marisol holding it to her chest while she looks at me with accusing eyes.

"You've had enough, don't ya think?" she says as she pointedly tips her head to the bottle of Jack Daniels I abandoned when she and Simon first arrived.

"She's right," Hank says from behind me.

I whirl around and glare at him. "Who's side are you on?"

He arches a brow. "Is Simon really here, Benny?"

"Yes. He's in bed."

"Then I'm on his side."

CHAPTER 9

Mama

"UNBELIEVABLE."

My lips twitch as I watch Benson stare down his brother. The two men look so much alike, it's unnerving. I can see why the police viewed Hank Green as a suspect early on in the investigation. It would make sense that Simon would get in a vehicle with his uncle.

But like the police and FBI, we quickly realized that Hank wasn't involved. He's too… good. Benson, on the other hand…

"Why don't we sit down and talk," I suggest. "I'm sure you both have a lot of questions."

Without waiting for them to respond, I return to the living room and sit on the couch. Maybe I should worry that they'll call the cops on me, but let's face it. If Benson was interested in doing that, he'd have done it already. Besides, he doesn't trust them any more than I do. They weren't the ones who found his son, after all.

When they both remain in the kitchen, I cross my arms over my chest. "Listen, I drove all the way from Atlantic City earlier, and I'm tired. If you've got questions, now is the time to ask them. Otherwise, I'm going to curl up here on this sofa and try to get some sleep."

Benson and Hank exchange a look, almost as if trying to figure out if I'm real.

News flash boys... I'm as real as they come.

Hank joins me in the living room first, while Benson stays near the counter, near his precious booze.

"Who are you?" Hank asks as he sits on the opposite end of the couch.

Rather than answer, I focus on Benson. The man is sexy as hell, I'll give him that. Muscular arms, rugged face. Too bad his personality sucks.

"I'd really prefer to only go through this once," I call out to him.

Benson stares a moment longer before grabbing the bottle of Jose Cuervo from the counter and striding toward me. He sits on the coffee table in front of the couch and twists off the cap.

Shoulda grabbed that bottle too.

After taking a swig, Benson swipes his mouth with his shirt sleeve. "Answer him."

"I already told you, my name is Marisol."

"Why does Simon call you Mama?" Benson asks.

"It's my road name. Everyone calls me Mama."

"Road name?"

I tilt my head and study him. Simon said his dad rides a motorcycle. Does he really not know what a road name is, or is he too drunk to put the pieces together?

"I'm a member of the Devil's Handmaidens MC," I tell him. "I'm the enforcer for the Atlantic City chapter."

"An MC?" Hank asks. "Seriously?"

"Got a problem with that, Hank?"

His eyes widen. "What? No, of course not. I've just never seen a woman biker."

"You need to get out more then," I deadpan and refocus on Benson. "Anyway, people call me Mama."

"Simon called you Mama," Benson says, his tone sad, and for the first time since I arrived, I feel sorry for the guy.

"He told me about his mom," I tell him. "I'm sorry for your loss. But you have to know, Simon didn't mean anything when he called me that. To him, it's just my name."

"Simon has a mom."

Oh boy.

Without thinking, I lean forward and grab Benson's hand. He tenses, but quickly relaxes when he realizes I'm not going to let go.

"He does," I agree. "He talks about her a lot. He misses her."

In fact, Simon wouldn't stop talking about his mom. I've heard so many stories over the last week that I feel like I know the woman.

"You look like her," Benson says quietly.

I rear back. Simon never mentioned that.

"That explains a lot."

"What do you mean?"

"Well, Simon kinda took to me pretty quickly. He could be around the other club members, but remained… withdrawn, I guess. But with me, he was fine. I just thought it was because I was the one who…"

"You were the one who what?" Benson prods.

Leaning back against the cushions, I try to find the right words. How do you tell a man that his son, who was kidnapped and held for six months, was also locked in a cage? How do you confirm what are likely his worst nightmares?

You just spit it out.

"I was the one who got him out of the cage."

Hank gasps, but Benson? He just nods, like he already knew.

"You don't seem surprised by that."

Benson huffs out a humorless laugh. "When you see the videos I've seen over the last six months, not much can surprise you."

"Videos?"

"What videos?"

Hank and I speak at the same time.

Benson takes a deep breath. "Special Agent Calhoun sent me videos of each auction."

"Auction?" Hank asks.

Now it's my turn to be confused. There was no mention in the reports of auction videos being shown to the family. Probably because it never should've happened.

"Okay, I think we need to back up here for a minute," I begin. "Why don't you tell me what you know?"

Benson shrugs. "Not much. Philly PD ran down leads, but never found anything. Then the FBI was called in, and their cyber-crimes division investigated. They were able to figure out that a trafficking ring had Simon, and that they were trying to sell him. But every auction ended prematurely. At least, that's what they told me. I never really knew if Simon had been sold or not because the videos cut off before a final bid was accepted."

"Dear God," Hank mutters. "Why didn't you tell me any of this, Benny?"

"What good would it have done?" Benson counters.

"I don't know," Hank exclaims. "But I'm your brother. If I'd have known wh—"

"What, Hank?" Benson snaps. "You would've what?"

Hank deflates. "I don't know."

"Exactly." Benson focuses on me. "I guess he wasn't sold."

Well, fuck.

"He was never transferred to a buyer, no," I say cautiously.

"Right. That's what I said."

"No. You said he wasn't sold," I clarify. "But…" I take a deep breath. "When we found Simon and the others, Simon was wearing a bracelet that marked him as sold."

"What?" he shouts as he jumps to his feet.

I stand and wrap my fingers around his forearms. "Benson, I need you to stay calm for me. Simon is in there sleeping, and the last thing he needs is to be woken up by your anger."

Benson glances toward the hall, his lips parted like he's going to argue, but then he sags back to the coffee table and nods. "Yeah, right. Okay."

"The important thing is that Simon is home. We found him in time, and he's safe right now."

"Right now?"

I sit on the edge of the couch and level my gaze on him. "Yeah, right now. We were able to eliminate a lot of the players, but the head of the trafficking ring is still out there."

"We need to call the FBI," Hank says.

Honestly, I'm surprised it took this long for the suggestion to come up. But I'm not surprised in the least that it wasn't Benson who made it. Benson doesn't trust law enforcement. And why would he? They let him down. It wasn't them who showed up with Simon. It was me.

"We can't do that," I say matter-of-factly.

"Why not?" Hank barks. "They need to know wh—"

"We can't call them because we don't know for sure that they aren't involved somehow."

"What?"

I sigh. "It's unclear, at this time, if the Philly PD or anyone at the FBI is being paid off by Flesh Dealer 2.0."

"Flesh De…" Benson shakes his head. "Did you say Flesh Dealer 2.0?"

"Yes."

"Who the fuck is that?"

"The person responsible for what happened to your son."

"What kind of name is Flesh Dealer 2.0?" Hank asks.

"A sick one," I suggest. "Look, I didn't name them. That's the screen name associated with all of the auctions, and the one that gets thrown around on the streets in regard to this particular ring."

"Do you know where to find them?"

"No," I admit. "But we will find them. I promise you that."

"And in the meantime, we're supposed to what? Keep this information to ourselves and hope like hell no one else comes for my son?"

"Benson, I will not let anything happen to Simon," I vow. "As long as I'm here, he's safe."

"But I don't know you!" he cries.

"I'm the woman who saved your son," I remind him. "I'm the woman who brought him home to you. Isn't that enough to gain me some trust?"

He stares at me for a long moment before turning to his brother. I follow his gaze and see Hank shrug.

When Benson returns his eyes to me, there's resignation in the blue depths.

"Fine. You have one week."

I release the breath I didn't realize I'd been holding. "One week. I can work with that."

"You better," he seethes. "Because that's all you're getting."

"You won't regret this, Benson. I promise."

CHAPTER 10

Benson

YOU WON'T REGRET THIS, *Benson. I promise.*

As I stare at the ceiling above my bed, I already regret it. I sent Hank home an hour ago, despite his protests, and now that I'm alone in the house with a woman I don't know, I have loads of regrets.

Not the least of which is that I didn't wish my son a happy birthday. Simon didn't seem to even realize it was his birthday, which is odd.

Is it? He's seven.

No, he's eight. And he's been held captive for six months. No shit he didn't realize it was his birthday.

I roll to my side and punch the pillow, but it does little to assuage my guilt. Flopping onto my other side, I try not to let my mind wander. And I fail miserably.

"Ben, please, promise me."

I lift Katie's frail hand and press a kiss to the back of it. The monitor beside the hospital bed that hospice set up in our living room beeps, letting me know that my wife is still alive, but fading.

"I can't, Katie girl," I tell her honestly. "I'll never love anyone the way I love you."

Katie laughs, which sends her into a coughing fit. I lift a glass of water to her lips and help her steady it so she can take a sip.

"Be serious, Ben."

"I am serious," I insist. "There isn't a woman in the world who—"

"Benson Green, stop." Katie's expression hardens. "I need to know that you won't shut yourself off after I'm gone. I need to know that you'll show our son that life is worth living, whether I'm here or not."

"Katie, I don't want to think about that."

"Well, neither do I. But I'm dying, Ben." She grips my hands as hard as she can. "I'm dying. Sooner rather than later."

"Noooooo!"

I bolt upright at the scream, snapping back into the present. Footsteps thud in the hallway, and I leap from my bed, race to the door, and throw it open to see Simon sprint past toward the living room.

I rush after him but halt in my tracks when I see the woman thrashing on the couch. Simon doesn't even hesitate. He goes right to the end of the sofa and calls out to her.

"Mama, wake up." He reaches out and taps her foot. "Mama, it's just a dream."

Simon continues to talk to her, to reassure her that she's okay, until she calms and curls in on herself, still fast asleep. He watches her for a few minutes before turning to me and frowning.

"She has nightmares," he says as if what just happened is completely normal.

"I, uh…" I thrust a hand through my hair. "I see that."

"Sorry she woke you up."

"It's okay. I wasn't sleeping."

"Well, I guess I better go back to bed," he says as he starts to walk past me.

"Hey, Simon."

He stops and faces me. "Yeah, Dad?"

I stoop to his level and tug him into my arms. He stiffens for a split-second but then
relaxes.

"I missed you," I tell him.

Simon remains silent but he holds on to my neck. My brain screams at me to pick him up and carry him to bed, but my body doesn't cooperate.

"Dad?"

"Yeah?"

"Are you gonna tuck me in or what?"

———

"What's all this?"

I look over my shoulder to see Marisol standing next to the counter. Her eyes are darting from one plate to the next, and doubt creeps in.

"Breakfast?"

"Are you asking me, or telling me?"

"Breakfast," I say with more assurance. "It's breakfast."

"Bacon, eggs, sausage, toast, biscuits and gravy, pancakes, and..." She points to the last platter. "Is that a birthday cake?"

"Yes." The excitement I felt when I called Hank and asked him to bring some groceries and a cake fades. "Maybe I went a little overboard," I say and toss the spatula I'm holding into the sink.

"I mean, is it your birthday?"

"No."

"Then why the birthday cake?"

I heave a sigh. "Because yesterday was Simon's birthday."

"Oh." Her shoulders deflate. "Shit."

"Whose birthday is it?"

Marisol and I both whirl around as Simon strolls into the kitchen, his Spiderman pajamas wrinkled from tossing and turning after he fell asleep. And yes, I stood in his doorway and watched him after tucking him in... all night.

I watched my son sleep all night, and it was... amazing.

"Hey, kiddo," I say with a smile. "Happy birthday!"

"It's not my birthday," he says.

Marisol shifts on her feet, looking uncomfortable. I get it because I feel uncomfortable too. Which is insane because he's my son, and I want to celebrate his birthday. What's so wrong or weird about that?

Fuck, I could use a drink.

I glance around the kitchen for the bottles of booze I bought yesterday but don't see them, and when my gaze lands back on Marisol, she's smirking.

"I dumped them out last night," she says, as if reading my mind. "Contrary to popular opinion, it's not always five o'clock somewhere."

A fresh wave of anger crashes over me. "You had no ri—"

She turns away from me to face Simon completely. "So, little man, I hear you're eight now," she exclaims.

"But it's not my birthday," he replies.

"But it was yesterday," she explains. "Your dad made this super awesome breakfast to celebrate, and guess what?"

"What?"

"He even got you a cake." Her excitement seems to light a fire in my son, and he grins. "I mean, cake for breakfast. Does it get any better than that?"

Simon slides his gaze to me. "Is it chocolate?"

"Of course, it is, kiddo," I assure him.

"Chocolate cake for breakfast!" he says, pumping his fist in the air.

"Go wash your hands and then we can eat," I instruct.

Simon races away, and I cross my hands over my chest to glare at Marisol.

"What?"

"How do you do that?"

"Do what?"

"How do you know just the right thing to say to him?"

She shrugs. "It's a gift."

"I'm being serious," I insist. "He's my son, but he might as well be a total stranger. I have no clue what he's thinking or feeling. One minute, he's leery around me and the next, he's fine. I don't know how to act around him."

Marisol grabs a piece of bacon and takes a bite. "I have years of experience with trafficking victims, Benson. It's what the Devil's Handmaidens specialize in." She shrugs, and I'm starting to realize that she does that a lot. "And it's been less than a day with Simon back. It's going to take time to get your footing with him and vice versa." She narrows her eyes at me. "But one thing I can tell you is that drinking your way through it isn't going to make it any easier."

I huff out a breath. "Ha. Maybe not for him, but it sure would for me."

"And how has that been working for you the last six months?"

"It's worked out fine," I snap, annoyance coursing through me.

"Right. Which is why you haven't worked since your wife died, you're burning through her life insurance, and you're shaking like a leaf right now because you need a drink." She smirks. "Seems to be working real fucking good."

"Ya know what?" I begin as I close the distance between us. "If you don't like how I handle things, you know where the damn door is."

She squares her shoulders and glares at me. "I'm not leaving until I know Simon is safe."

"Safe from what?"

"Anything… including you."

CHAPTER 11
Mama

"HOW'S IT GOING?"

I tuck the phone between my shoulder and ear as I pace the length of the driveway. Harlow has been texting me all day for an update, and this is the first chance I've had to call and give her one.

"The man is infuriating."

My president chuckles. "That good, huh?"

"Before I get into how good it's fucking going, how come no one told me that it was Simon's birthday yesterday? Surely that was in the records Nico hacked somewhere."

"It was his birthday?"

"Yes!" I exclaim, and when the woman walking her dog down the sidewalk slows to stare at me, I glare at her until she starts walking again. "Fucking Karen," I mutter.

"What?"

"Nothing," I say, shaking my head. "And yes, it was his birthday. I feel horrible that we didn't know that."

"It sucks, Mama, but there's nothing you can do about it now."

"Benson made him a huge breakfast, cake included."

"Okay."

"And then we went to the toy store, where he dropped a few hundred bucks on whatever Simon wanted."

"Okay."

"And now that we're back at the house, they're playing video games and eating ice cream."

"You're saying all of this like it's a bad thing."

"It is a bad thing," I insist. "Benson is acting like he can buy his son's trauma away."

"Mama, he's acting like a father who hasn't seen his son in six months and just wants some normalcy for him."

I groan. "But nothing about this situation is normal. Simon was held captive, in a cage, and then auctioned off to the highest bidder. His life is never going to be the same as it was before all that."

"Well, you and I know that. And I'm guessing Benson does too. But you've gotta give him time."

"I don't have time. Simon doesn't have time. Flesh Dealer 2.0 is gonna come for him, Har. Or the buyer will. Either way, this whole situation is fucked."

"Which is why you're there, remember?" She sighs, and I can hear the faint sounds of slot machines pinging in the background, telling me she's at Devil's Double Down. "Look, why don't you bring them both back to Atlantic City, and they can stay at the clubhouse? That way this doesn't all fall on you."

"Is that an order or a suggestion?"

"It's an option."

"Normally, it's one I'd be all for, but I started this, so I have to finish it."

"You did not start this, Mama," Harlow snaps. "None of this is your fault."

Not wanting to get into this right now, I change the subject. "How are things there?"

"Don't think I don't know what you're doing." Harlow takes a deep breath. "But I'll let it slide… for now."

"How are things there?" I repeat, essentially pleading the fifth.

"Things are fine here. The casino is still raking in the dough, and Malachi and Nico just took on another case in Europe."

"Europe?"

"Some socialite went missing while on vacation in Italy. As you can imagine, her parents are very worried, and paying out the ass for them to find her."

"Suspicion of trafficking?"

"Always," she says with a chuckle. "But, no, not really. Based on her social media accounts, she's a spoiled brat who hates having to check in with Mommy and Daddy. The retrieval team will get there and most likely have her in hand within a day. And then they'll bring her back to the US, kicking and screaming. But she'll be home, and the clients will be happy."

"Glad it's them and not me."

"You and me both, sister."

"Well, look, I should get back inside, make sure Benson hasn't dipped into a secret stash of liquor," I say, only half teasing.

"He has a secret stash?"

"I don't know," I admit. "I dumped all the bottles I found after he went to bed. But he's a drinker who's had a shit year, so it wouldn't surprise me."

"Good luck with that."

"Thanks, Prez," I say dryly.

"Call me if you need anything," she instructs. "And Mama?"

"Yeah?"

"Be careful. Keep your eyes and ears to the ground. Expect anything."

"Always."

After disconnecting the call, I shove my cell into my back

pocket and make my way back inside. Simon and Benson are still sitting on the couch, game controllers in hand, and they're laughing and playing as if nothing at all out of the ordinary is going on.

"So, boys, do you still have room for dinner?"

Neither acknowledges my presence, which only serves to piss me off. Like a toddler throwing a tantrum, I stomp to the television and turn it off, successfully getting their full attention.

"Hey, Mama," Simon whines.

"What the hell?" Benson demands.

Crossing my arms over my chest, I cock my hip. "I asked you both a question."

"What?"

"Are you hungry, or did the ice cream ruin your appetite for dinner?"

Benson rolls his eyes and reaches for his mug on the coffee table. He takes a sip as he leans back against the cushions.

"I'm not hungry."

"I'm always hungry."

They both speak at the same time. "Well, which is it? Am I making something for dinner or not?"

"You can cook?" Benson asks.

"I can do a lot of things."

"She's pretty good, but Giggles is better," Simon adds his two cents.

"Thanks, little man," I say ruefully. "Although you're right. Giggles is better. But I can make a pretty good lasagna."

I should be good at it, considering it was the first thing my mom taught my sister and I to cook. She drilled the recipe into both of us, claiming that any Italian woman worth their salt should be able to make lasagna as if their life depended on it.

"Yum!" Simon exclaims. "I love lasagna."

Benson, on the other hand, stares at me like I've grown a second head.

"Then lasagna it is. That is, if it's okay with your dad."

"It's, uh…" Benson clears his throat. "Yeah, it's fine."

"Good. Now the question is, do you have everything I need to make it?"

"Probably not." Benson tosses the game controller onto the couch next to him before standing. "But I can run to the store."

Suspicion creeps in at his eagerness. "Why don't we all go?"

"Oh, uh, no, that's okay. I'm gonna take the Harley. I could use the fresh air."

We lock eyes, each of us daring the other to back down. I know he's lying, and he knows I know. But Simon is present, and I refuse to argue in front of him.

"Okay, if you're sure," I say, caving. "Do you need me to write you out a list?"

"If you just text it to me, that'll work."

I take out my cell and type out a quick list before hitting send. His cell phone pings with the notification.

"Might want to save my info to your contacts. Ya know, so you don't ignore any more important calls."

Benson narrows his eyes. "You just couldn't resist, could you?"

"Nope."

"Should I save it under 'Marisol' or 'Mama'?" he asks.

"How about 'not a reporter'?" I sass.

"'Crazy lady' it is then," he snaps back.

So much for not arguing.

"Can I go with you?" Simon asks, breaking the tension in the room.

Benson smiles at his son. "Not this time, kiddo. I'll be quick, I promise."

"But I wanna go."

Benson glances at me as if to silently ask for help, but he's on his own with this one. I want no part of him lying to Simon so he can get more booze.

"Next time."

"But Da-ad," Simon singsongs.

"No," Benson snaps, his temper flaring, and Simon shrinks into the cushions of the couch. "We'll go for a ride tomorrow, okay?"

"Yeah, fine."

Benson practically runs out of the living room, through the kitchen, and into the garage. The unmistakable rumble of a motorcycle filters inside, and jealousy courses through me.

I wish I had my bike. I could use some fresh fucking air, too.

CHAPTER 12
Benson

WATER CASCADES over my head as I rinse the shampoo from my hair. After dinner, which was mouth-wateringly incredible, Simon took a bubble bath, leaving me alone with Marisol. The tension between us was so thick, I knew I had to find an excuse to get away from her.

As soon as Simon emerged from the bathroom, I suggested we watch a movie. But once I got it playing, I made my escape. Claiming I needed a shower wasn't my most innovative lie, but it seemed to do the trick.

Or it didn't. Something tells me that Marisol is far more observant than I want her to be.

I reach past the shower curtain and lift the bottle of Jack Daniels off the ledge of the tub. After a moment's hesitation, I tip it to my lips and take a healthy swig. I've been shaky all day, and as soon as Marisol mentioned going to the store, I jumped at the chance.

I desperately needed a drink, which is why I'm confused as all hell that it's not calming me like I thought it would.

Because Simon is home, and you know you need to stop.

I chug some more in a vain attempt to chase my thoughts away. It fails to work.

It never worked, dumbass. It just made you think it did.

After setting the bottle down, I leisurely finish my shower. By the time I'm clean—not that I was all that dirty—the water is cold, and I'm shivering. At least the shaking isn't related to my alcohol intake.

Throwing the curtain aside, I step out onto the cold tile and make a mental note to put in heated flooring. There's a laundry list of things I want to do with this house, and I started a to-do list back when Simon and I moved in, but then he was kidnapped. And I have no clue where that list is now.

I wrap a towel around my waist, having to hold it closed with my hand, and move to the door to see if I can hear any movement. Relieved when the movie is all that reaches my ears, I open the door and turn to walk to my room. As I pass by Simon's bedroom, movement catches my eye, and I stop in the doorway.

Marisol is pulling the comforter over Simon, who appears sound asleep. I watch her watch him, and my late wife's voice sounds in my head.

Ben, please, promise me.

An ache forms in my chest at the intrusive thought. Katie eventually got me to promise her I wouldn't totally shut down after she died, but I don't think this is what she had in mind. Hell, it's not what I have in mind.

Marisol is annoying and bitchy and bossy and… really good with my son. She's also gorgeous, judgmental, and carries weapons.

And really fucking good with Simon.

She bends to press a kiss to Simon's forehead and when she turns around, she jumps.

"What are you doing?" she demands in a harsh whisper.

"I thought you were watching a movie."

She quietly walks to the door and, leaving the light on, pushes me out into the hall. "We were, but he fell asleep."

"I would've carried him in."

"Are you sure you could've done that and stayed upright?" she asks, her brow arched.

Forgetting about needing to hold my towel closed, I throw up my hands. "What's that supposed to mean?"

And for the first time since I opened my door to see her standing on my porch, Marisol is silent. More specifically, she's silently staring at my cock, which is now fully exposed because the damn towel dropped to the floor.

I know I should pick it up, cover myself. But I can't. My body won't obey the commands my brain is screaming at it.

Bullshit! Your brain isn't screaming anything but 'fuck yes'.

"Marisol?"

No response, but her hand clutches her neck as she swallows.

"Crazy lady?" I try and still, nothing. "Mama!"

Her head whips up, and her eyes are large pools of... lust? "Huh?"

"What did you mean about me not being able to stay upright?"

"I..." She swallows again. "For the love of..." She bends to pick up the towel and slams it against my chest, forcing me to grab it. "Go put some clothes on before I..."

I grin. "Before you what?"

Am I flirting? Is she?

Why am I questioning this? Just go with it, dipshit. It's been a long damn time since you—

"Clothes," she barks. "Now."

Marisol storms past me toward the living room. I glance down at my dick and roll my eyes. Of course, this is when it chooses to come to life. And for a woman who infuriates me, no less.

She wasn't infuriating you a second ago.

She's infuriated me from the moment I met her. All of twenty-four hours ago, give or take a few minutes.

Ben, please, promise me.

Pretty sure this isn't what Katie had in mind.

Pissed off at myself for even entertaining such thoughts, I storm the rest of the way to my room and close the door. I toss the towel into the hamper in the corner before rummaging through my dresser for a pair of sleep pants. I'd prefer to sleep naked, but that's not happening. But I don't bother with a shirt.

It's my fucking house, and if she doesn't like it, she's welcome to leave.

Yeah, tough guy… go tell that to her face.

With a determination to reclaim my own home, I throw open my door and stride down the hall to the bathroom. I snag the bottle of Jack Daniels I left on the tub ledge and down several gulps.

I need fortification to keep up this determination. Sue me.

The whiskey warms me, and I carry it into the living room, where I stop in my tracks at the sight I'm greeted by.

Marisol has her back to me, and she's bent over, digging through her bag. The black thong she's wearing is nestled between her ass cheeks, and my mouth waters.

Whoever said whiskey dick is a thing never went over a year without sex.

"Son of a bitch."

CHAPTER 13

Mama

"SON OF A BITCH."

I whirl around with a gasp at Benson's harsh tone, startled to realize I'm not alone. After he'd shut his bedroom door, I decided to quickly change, but apparently, I'm not all that quick. Our eyes are locked, but I see the bottle of Jack Daniels in his hand, and that breaks the spell he seems to have put me under.

"Seriously?" I snark. "You're drinking?"

His eyebrows shoot up to his hairline. "That's what you're focused on right now?"

Man's got a point.

And a cock… a very rigid cock.

Benson palms his dick through his cotton sleep pants. "Nice of you to notice."

"What?"

"My cock," he says. "My *very rigid cock*." He does his best to mimic my voice, and embarrassment floods my system because I realize I spoke my thoughts out loud.

"What are you doing?"

"I was coming out here to talk to you," he says as if I'm

not standing here almost naked. "But I'm gonna need you to put some clothes on first."

A groan barrels out of me. "You're impossible," I snap as I turn around to dig shorts out of my bag.

As I'm rifling through my clothes and various weapons, the smell of shampoo and soap invades my senses. My nipples pebble, and I close my eyes.

A large hand settles against my spine, and I shiver involuntarily. "I'm not impossible," Benson murmurs as he leans over me.

The whiskey on his breath reminds me that I'm supposed to be mad at him, but my body doesn't seem to care. I slowly straighten, and turn to face him, all thought of clothes abandoned.

"You hate me," I say.

His eyes darken for a moment before he shakes his head. "I don't hate you. I just don't like you very much."

"Then what is this?" I ask, moving my hand back and forth between us.

Benson tips the Jack Daniels to his lips, but before he can take a drink, I grab it and take a swing of my own. He arches a brow but doesn't comment.

"Benson, your son is right down the hall," I remind him.

What the hell? Why does it sound like I'm actually entertaining the idea of fucking him?

Probably because, against my far superior judgment, I am. I've been under so much stress lately, and I know it's only going to get worse. Taking a little time to decompress isn't the worst idea I've ever had.

"Sounds like you're open to the idea of this, of us," he replies.

"And if I am?"

He grabs my hand and brings it to his crotch. "Clearly, I am too."

"But you don't like me."

"And you don't like me," he says as he leans close to my ear. "We don't have to like each other to fuck."

"What about after?" I ask, fighting like hell to keep my wits about me.

"What about it?"

"I'm not leaving until I know Simon is safe."

"Okay."

"This will change nothing."

"Good."

"This is a terrible idea."

He threads his fingers through my curly hair and cups my face. "The worst idea."

"It's just a little stress relief," I say, my tone breathy.

"Agreed."

Out of arguments, I give in to my baser instincts and jump up, giving Benson no choice but to catch me. As I crash my mouth against his, I wrap my legs around his waist. I'm gonna pay for this later, but I simply don't care.

Benson's tongue darts out and he teases the seam of my lips, demanding entry. I swirl my tongue with his, deepening the kiss. I'm dimly aware of him carrying me, of our surroundings changing, but it doesn't dawn on me where we're going until cool air hits my skin.

Breaking the kiss, I look around and spot his Harley, which is parked in his garage. When I return my attention to him, he's sporting a wicked grin.

"Still good?" he asks, and I hate that my heart melts the tiniest bit at the question.

We might both agree that this is a bad idea, but I know if I told him to stop, he would. I have no damn clue how I know. Gut feeling, I guess.

"Never better," I reply, desperation bleeding into the words.

He seals his lips over mine again and carries me the rest of the way to his bike. After he sets me on my feet, we break apart and strip as fast as we can.

"Turn around," he commands, his nostrils flaring.

And giving in to my inner hussy, I obey without hesitation.

"Brace yourself on the seat."

Again, I obey. Glancing over my shoulder, I watch as he steps close to my back, his dick in his hand. He's hard as a rock, and my pussy throbs. He nudges at my entrance and locks his eyes on mine.

"Please tell me you're on the pill," he growls, as if pausing to ask causes him physical pain.

"I am."

Benson thrusts forward, and I almost lose my footing. His cock stretches me, fills me so completely. I dig my nails into the leather of the seat, glad I keep them short because it would be a shame to damage such a fine machine.

Flesh slaps against flesh as his hips fly, and I push back to meet him, thrust for thrust.

"Holy fuck," he groans. "It's been too damn long."

Benson pulls out and spins me around before lifting me into his arms and carrying me toward the wall. I lose my breath as my back hits the plaster, and he's inside of me before I can catch it again.

Wrapping my legs around his hips, I absorb his weight as he pistons in and out, in and out. His cock drags along my inner walls, and as amazing as it feels, it's not gonna get me off.

"Clit," I breathe. "Need you to touch my clit."

I've never had a problem vocalizing what I like, and judging by his wide eyes, Benson isn't used to that. But he listens, and that's what matters.

He presses his thumb against my clit and rubs slow circles around it, all the while not letting up with his thrusts. The combination of sensations is intoxicating, and exactly what I need.

"Ah, yeah," I moan as I throw my head back, ignoring the sting of pain as it hits the wall. "Just like that."

Benson maintains his pace as he presses his body closer and snags my lips between his teeth. He nibbles and licks, and as the pleasure builds, he grunts with exertion.

Thrust.

Rub.

Nibble.

Lick.

Grunt.

We fuck as if our lives depend on it, and who knows? Maybe they do. Or maybe it's just our sanity. Whatever it is, I'm loving it.

"C'mon, Mama," he grinds out between nibbles. "Come for me," he commands.

Benson commands, and I obey. That seems to be the way of things with us. At least when we're naked.

I moan out my release, my pussy pulsing around his cock, and he follows me over the ledge. I pulse, he throbs, and stress dissipates. It's a beautiful thing.

He holds me up for a few moments after the pleasure abates, but when he lowers me to the floor and steps back, things become less... beautiful.

And just like that, everything has changed.

Or nothing.

Either way, fucking Benson was a huge fucking fucktastic mistake.

CHAPTER 14
Benson

"I'M STILL NOT LEAVING."

I grab my sleep pants off the garage floor, as well as her discarded thong, before straightening to face her. The moment the sex ended, regret reared its ugly head. I toss her panties at her, but she makes no move to catch them.

"I know."

Turning away from her, I pull my pants on and mentally berate myself for being an idiot. Why couldn't I have just masturbated like a normal person?

Because you're far from normal.

"Are you gonna want me to start calling you Mr. Green now?" she asks, her voice quiet but her tone filled with sass.

I whirl around. "What?"

Marisol shrugs. "You're acting weird. Typically, fucking brings people closer, not farther apart."

"Is that what you thought would happen?"

She throws her head back and laughs, which pisses me off. When she sobers, she levels her gaze on me.

"You're a jackass, *Mr. Green.* If I remember right, I was the one throwing out all the reasons this was a bad idea, which you agreed with, by the way. But somehow, we both shut down all those reasons and did it anyway." She pulls her panties on, which is pointless for all the skin they cover. "I had no expectations other than to get off. I thought you felt the same." She crosses her arms over her tits, and I almost swallow my tongue. "Maybe it's you who thought something more would come from it."

"Would you stop?" I bark.

"Stop what?"

"That." I wave my hand in her direction. "Looking like that. Stop it."

"I'll stop when you stop," she counters vehemently.

Resisting the urge to scream, I stride past her, mumbling, "This is ridiculous."

I move through the kitchen and living room, then down the hall. And she's only steps behind me.

"Quit following me," I snap.

"Quit acting like a—"

I stop to face her, expecting her to finish, but she has her lips pursed and her head cocked instead.

"What?"

"Hear that?" she asks as she thrusts her arms into her tank top.

When the hell did she grab that?

"Hear what?"

A faint whimper reaches my ears.

"That," she says as she pushes past me toward Simon's room.

My son is thrashing around in his bed, and the comforter is twisted around his small body. Frozen and unsure what to do, I stand by while Marisol races forward and methodically tries to untangle him, all while dodging his flying hands and feet.

Once he's free, she sits on the mattress and pulls him into her arms to cradle him, much like one would with a baby. It takes several minutes, but he calms as she rocks back and forth, murmuring assurances to him.

Marisol extricates herself from him and covers him back up. She stares at him for a moment and then says, "Sleep tight, little man."

When she reaches me, she grabs my arm and drags me out into the hall. "He has nightmares," she finally says, as if I couldn't figure that out on my own.

A sense of déjà vu washes over me. These two… they have more in common than they realize. And I've never felt more like an outsider in my own life than I do right now.

"So do you," I say absently.

Her expression sharpens. "What?"

Shit.

Can't take it back now.

"You have nightmares too."

"So?"

"It's just…" I heave a sigh. "Last night, you had one, and Simon was able to calm you down."

"He what?"

"I heard a yell and came out of my room to see what it was," I explain. "I thought it was Simon, but he was running past my room toward the couch, and then he just… calmed you down. It was like he'd done it before and knew exactly what would work."

"Oh." Marisol averts her gaze. "Sorry."

"Jesus, you don't have to be sorry," I mutter, annoyed with myself that I made her feel that way. "A lot of people have nightmares."

"Do you?" she asks, and she sounds genuinely interested. Which is crazy.

Right?

"All the time," I admit.

The sound of rustling blankets drifts into the hallway, and I peak into Simon's room to see him rolling over. He doesn't appear distressed, so I return my attention back to the conversation at hand.

"Let's go sit," I suggest. "I don't want to wake him up."

"Oh, um, okay."

Seriously? Now she's unsure and shy?

"I'll even go put on a shirt," I tease, suddenly desperate for things to be normal. Whatever the fuck that is. "And you need to put on pants."

I turn to go to my room, but don't miss her chuckle. Her footsteps thud on the hardwood as she heads in the opposite direction.

Five minutes and a mental pep talk later, I'm sitting on one end of the couch, and she's on the other end. We're facing each other, but neither of us is making any move to speak.

"Alcohol would make this much easier," I finally say to break the silence.

She narrows her eyes. "No, it wouldn't. Alcohol makes things worse." She fidgets with her hands. "So much worse," she adds, almost as an afterthought.

"There's a story there," I say.

"Yeah, and not one I want to talk about."

"Okay. Then let's talk about Simon," I suggest. "He seems to be the one commonality between us."

"Yeah, probably."

"So?"

"He's a great kid."

"He is," I agree. "But I'm probably biased."

"Nah. He really is. Own that shit, Benson. Not every parent can make the same statement."

"I wish I could take all the credit. But Katie…"

She keeps her eyes trained on mine, as if trying to determine if I'm going to lose my shit. But somehow, I don't. It's weird, but the thought of talking to Marisol about Katie, the thought of talking about Katie at all, isn't filling me with unbearable anguish.

"Simon talked a lot about her the week he was at the club-house. She sounds like she was an amazing mother."

I smile fondly. "She was. The best, actually. She deserves all the credit where Simon is concerned."

She laughs, and it sounds… pretty.

Ben, please, promise me.

Dammit!

"I'm sure she deserves most of the credit," she teases. "But you were there too. He talked about you just as much as he did about Katie."

"Oh yeah?"

"Wanna know how I won him over?"

"Please," I practically beg. "Maybe I can use whatever tricks you have up your sleeve."

"He'll come around, Benson." Marisol scoots closer, but not too close. "He just needs time. And it wouldn't hurt to get him into counseling. I know some of the things he went through, but there's a lot he's keeping to himself." She straightens and smiles. "But, back to my tricks… it was my Harley."

"What?"

"He wanted to ride with me on my Harley," she says simply. "When we're on a rescue mission, we typically use our vans for transportation. More room and all that. I was set to go in the van with him and let someone ride my Harley back to the clubhouse. Which, if you know anything about bikers, that doesn't happen. But I was prepared to do that, for Simon. But then he heard the rumble of the Harley, and he lit up."

"That doesn't surprise me. When Simon was a baby, he was not a good sleeper. He'd cry for hours. Katie and I were at our wit's end until one particularly bad night. I was working late, and she was struggling to get him calmed down. It was summer, and I'd ridden my Harley to work. The way Katie told it, as soon as he heard the rumble of my

Harley when I pulled into our garage, he calmed right down. From that night on, any time he was fussy, I'd fire up the bike until he fell asleep."

"And it worked?"

"Like a charm."

She whistles appreciatively. "My kinda kid."

"Yeah, me too."

Silence follows, but it's not uncomfortable, and I don't feel the need to fill it. I miss this. Sharing stories, talking to someone. It feels good.

Which makes me feel bad.

Doesn't it?

Ben, please, promise me.

"We should probably try to get some sleep," she says after several minutes.

"Yeah, we should."

I push myself up and shift from one foot to the other.

"Benson? What is it?"

"Thank you," I blurt as I face her. "I don't think I've told you that yet but... thank you for bringing my son back to me."

"It's what I do," she says flippantly.

"Don't."

"Don't what?"

"Don't minimize it. What you do, what your club does? There aren't many people in the world who would even give a damn. But you? You've made it your life."

"I'm all too aware of those who don't give a damn," she says, but before I can question what she means, she continues. "But you're welcome. I'm glad I was able to get him home."

I nod with a smile. "G'night, Mama."

She grins. "It's Mama now?"

"It suits you."

CHAPTER 15
Mama

PING.

Ping.

Ping.

Ping.

Twisting on the couch, I grumble as I reach to grab my cell phone off the coffee table. My back aches, as do my lady bits. One ache is good and the other, well, sucks.

"This better be good," I mumble as I pull up the text messages coming through.

Unknown: You have something that belongs to me.

Unknown: I want it back.

Unknown: Don't make this harder than it has to be, Mari.

I bolt upright, and my head spins at the sudden movement. There is only one person left in this world who calls me Mari.

Unknown: Tsk-Tsk, Mari. Philly might be a big city, but you can't hide what's mine.

Switching out of the texts, I hit the speed dial for Harlow, then the speakerphone icon. She answers on the third ring.

"This better be good," she says by way of greeting.

Great minds and all that.

"We've got a problem."

"Mama?"

"Yes, it's Mama," I snap. "C'mon, Prez. I need your brain firing on all cylinders."

"What's the problem?"

"Flesh Dealer 2.0 has my cell number."

"Well, that's not exactly surprising."

"They know I'm in Philadelphia."

"Who knows you're in Philadelphia?"

I whip my head to the side and see Benson standing at the end of the couch, rubbing a hand over his bare chest.

"Why are you sneaking up on me?" I snap.

"Mama, who the fuck are you talking to?" Harlow barks, concern lacing her tone.

"No one."

"No one?" Benson repeats incredulously. "Who is that?" He nods to my cell phone, which I'm regretting putting on speaker.

In my defense, it's not even six in the morning, and I thought I was the only one awake.

"Benson Green, this is Harlow, my Prez," I say, lifting the cell. "Harlow, Benson's here now."

"Who knows you're in Philadelphia?" Benson repeats.

"Nice to meet you too," Harlow snaps.

"Answer me, Marisol," he growls.

"Marisol, is it?" Harlow taunts. "Most people call you Mama. But I guess that would be a tad weird, all things considered."

"All what things?" I ask.

"Well, you were acting as a surrogate mother to his son for a week and probably still are, and his real mother is… Ya know what, never mind. It's too early for this shit."

"He called me Mama last night," I grumble, and immediately slap my hand over my mouth.

Way too fucking early.

"Wait a second," Harlow says. "He called you… Aw, Mama, really? You slept with him?"

"Why is that a bad thing?" Benson demands as if this isn't the most ridiculous conversation in the history of conversations, or as if it's the most important thing at the moment.

"Because you're the dad of a victim. And a drinker, if police records are to be believed. Mama deserves better than that." She sighs. "No offense," she tacks on.

"Offense taken," he snaps as he flops beside me and yanks my cell out of my hand. "And why are you looking at my arrest records? That's an invasion of privacy!"

"We had to be sure you were a good guy," Harlow says unapologetically. "It wouldn't have been good for Simon if we saved him from one evil only to send him into the arms of another, now would it?"

"Oh, well, no," he capitulates.

"Can we get back on track, please?" I groan.

"Did you sleep with him, Mama?" Harlow asks.

"No."

"Yes."

Benson and I speak at the same time. I press my hands to my temples in an effort to stave off the headache I know is coming.

"You're right, Mama, we need to get back on track," Harlow says as if the whole sex topic was never raised. "Are you going to answer him, or should I? He deserves to know."

Benson stares at me expectantly, but I can't spit the words out. Sensing this, Harlow does it for me.

"Flesh Dealer 2.0 knows she's there," she says.

His eyes darken. "What?"

I heave a sigh. "Simon's captor knows I'm here."

"Mama, I'm gonna go so you can deal with Daddy dearest there. If you need us, call. And if you need to come back to Atlantic City, let me know ahead of time, and I'll send you an escort."

"Okay, Prez. Thanks."

"Anytime," she trills before hanging up.

I take my cell back from Benson and toss it onto the coffee table. He remains still, quiet, and very angry looking.

"So, yeah. This isn't good."

He lunges to his feet and begins to pace. "Why do I get the feeling that there's a lot you're not telling me?"

Because there is.

"I don't know," I lie.

"Bullshit," he snaps. "This is my son we're talking about. You can't just tell me that this Flesh Dealer two point whatever knows you're in Philadelphia and expect me to sit back and wait to see what happens."

"Just because I'm here, doesn't mean that I'm—"

"Stop!" he shouts. "Stop feeding me some shit story that you reserve for the family members of victims. Tell me what's going on."

Ping.

Ping.

I go to grab my cell, but Benson beats me to it. He scrolls through the texts, and his face pales. As if on autopilot, he closes the distance between us and lowers himself to the coffee table.

Benson hands me the phone, and when I hesitate to take it, he lifts my hand and slams the cell into it.

"Care to explain that… Mari?"

CHAPTER 16

Benson

"DON'T CALL ME THAT."

I glare at Marisol as I use every ounce of willpower I possess not to puke. She, on the other hand, is wearing an expression of defeat. And for some reason, that hurts almost as much as being lied to. She's been a firecracker since we met, but two texts are all it takes to break her. I don't like it.

"Is that shit true?" I ask, nodding toward the phone in her hand.

The messages scroll through my brain on a never-ending loop.

Unknown: C'mon, Mari. We're not kids anymore. I don't like to play games.

Unknown: Return what's mine and we'll call it even, little sis… despite the obscene amount of money you've cost me.

"Is. It. True?" I seethe.

When she nods, I have to grip the edge of the table for support.

"But I wasn't completely sure," she pushes out. "I had my suspicions, and those texts confirm them."

"Explain."

She rises from the couch and begins to pace, wearing a path just like I was a few minutes ago.

"When I was ten, my sister, Martina, left me home alone to go out on a date. She was supposed to be babysitting, but she didn't care." She flaps her hand as if realizing how insignificant that detail is. "I remember when she walked out the door, I thought that she better get home before our parents because if she didn't, they'd kill her." She pauses, but only briefly. "But she didn't come home at all, and no one, including her date, seemed to know where she was. There was an investigation, and just like you, my parents organized vigils and searches. But she was never found. Then one day, the FBI showed up at our door to show my parents a video. It was an auction, like the one you saw of Simon. And the online handle of the person running it was Flesh Dealer. My sister was one of many being auctioned off."

"Jesus," I mutter, acutely aware of how her parents felt watching that, how she must have felt. "I didn't know."

"Of course, you didn't," she says. "No one does, other than Harlow. The rest of the story isn't exactly shit I'm proud of."

"Okay."

"Anyway, Martina wasn't lucky like Simon. No one rescued her. She was sold off. I didn't know that until years later. And my parents never knew. They blamed me for letting her leave, even though I was only ten and Martina was sixteen. When time passed and there were no more leads, they turned to alcohol and drugs and... died before the truth of it all came out."

What kind of parent blames their child for that? And then to turn to drugs and alcohol instead of taking care of the child they still had...

You turned to alcohol.

Now her aversion to my drinking makes sense.

"Before they died, they had her declared dead. You see, all we had was that one video. We assumed the worst, and the FBI never corrected us. I don't know if they knew the truth, but I suspect they didn't. If they did, none of what's happening now would be happening."

"And the truth is?" I prod.

"Turns out Stockholm Syndrome is a real thing," she says with a chuckle, but there's no humor in it. "She fell for the man who bought her, and together they took down the original Flesh Dealer."

"I mean, that's a good thing, right?"

"On the surface, yes," she admits. "But by this time, Martina was so fucking warped in the head, she turned on the man who bought her. Killed him and started to build her own empire. She became Flesh Dealer 2.0."

"I thought you said you had suspicions, but it sounds like you knew."

"It's complicated, Benson."

"More complicated than what you've already told me?"

"When it comes to human trafficking and my sister, it can always get more complicated." Marisol stops pacing to sit back on the couch. "I was fifteen when our parents died. A real Romeo and Juliet situation, if you get my drift." I nod, confirming that I do, and resist the urge to haul her into my arms and soothe away the pain. "I had no other family, so I was put into foster care. When I aged out, I started working as a waitress in Atlantic City. One day, a woman walked in, and she seemed very out of place. The place was a dive, and she was dressed to the nines, ya know? Anyway, it was Martina. She came to recruit me. There was never any mention of auctions or anything, just the very basics. I turned her away. And then was approached by Harlow, who'd overheard a lot of the conversation. She did manage to recruit me that day, into the DHMC."

"Sounds like the club came at exactly the right time."

"They really did. And I made the club's mission my life. Eliminate the skin trade. I was always looking for Martina, but she fell off the radar. I knew she was out there somewhere, but there was never anything close that I could link to her."

"Why didn't you go to the cops?" I ask, genuinely curious.

"Because Benson. If they caught her, and that was a big if, she'd likely walk. But if I catch her?" She shakes her head. "She's not walking away from that."

"Okay, so years went by, and you couldn't find her," I say, trying to get back on track.

"Right. Until this past year, I'd almost given up hope of ever finding her. And then we took out the Ricci Crime Family, and that opened up the east coast for Martina to move in and take over the territory."

"I remember that on the news," I say, admiration in my words. "That was you?"

For the first time since starting her story, Marisol grins. "It was. Of course, Harlow is now shacked up with Malachi Ricci, and Peppermint, our VP, is with Nico Ricci, Malachi's cousin. But that's—"

"Another story for another time," I interrupt.

"Exactly," she confirms. "Please don't think the worst of them. Malachi and Nico... they aren't like the rest we took out. They're good men."

"Okay."

"So, yeah, once the Ricci Crime Family was out, the online auctions like the one Martina was sold in started back up. We chased lead after lead, but we were always too late. Every video you saw of Simon, we saw too. Those auctions ended because Nico hacked into the system and put an end to them."

I release a pent-up breath. This is so much more complicated than I could have imagined.

"The day we rescued Simon and the others, we got a tip from a woman. We were never able to trace who or where it came from, but it was the break we needed. Finally, we weren't too late."

"Damn," I say with a sigh. "How are you even remotely sane?"

"Who says I am?" Before I have a chance to respond, not that I would touch that question with a ten-foot pole, she returns to the topic of her sister. "When I saw that the person running the auctions with Simon was using the handle Flesh Dealer 2.0, of course, I suspected Martina. But I never had proof, and fuck, I wanted to be wrong. Deep down, I hoped my sister was dead, the life as a trafficker having taken her out. I don't know what kind of person that makes me, but there you have it."

"It doesn't make you a horrible person," I insist, and it doesn't. Not by a long shot. "It makes you human. I know she's your sister, but if she is Flesh Dealer 2.0, which it seems like she is, she doesn't deserve to breathe the same air as the rest of us."

Marisol half smiles. "I'd give anything for it not to be her, Benson. I swear to you, I would. But those texts... they pretty much confirm it. She's the only person still alive who calls me Mari. Everyone else in my life knows I'll take my ax to them if they do."

"Your ax?"

"Oh, right. You only know about the knife and gun." She leans over the end of the couch and when she straightens, she's holding, you guessed it, an ax. "Never leave home without it."

"What the fuck, Mama?"

"Oh, it's Mama again?"

"Shut up."

"Look, when it comes to my job, I never take chances," she explains. "And keeping Simon safe? I've made that my job."

"So this isn't the normal victim family treatment?"

"No, it's not. I'm the enforcer. I make sure club rules are followed, and protect the patch, no matter what. I'm the badass of the group."

"The rest of them aren't badass?"

"If you value your life, never ask that question again. Ever."

"All badasses. Got it."

"Good man."

"I try."

"Daddy, what did you do?"

Marisol and I both jump to our feet and turn to face Simon, who's wearing a very concerned expression on his face.

"What do you mean, kiddo?" I ask as I walk toward him.

Simon points toward the woman behind me. "Mama doesn't take out the ax unless she's really, really mad." He grins at her. "Isn't that what you told me?"

"It is exactly what I told you, little man," she says with a laugh. "But I'm not mad. Not at your dad anyway. I was just showing it to him."

"Like show and tell?"

"Just like that."

"Oh, okay." Simon rubs his eyes. "So, what's for breakfast?"

CHAPTER 17
Mama

SAVED BY THE... kid?

As I stand in the shower, I tip my head back and let the water splash over my face. I've never sat down with anyone and told them my story, my sister's story. Harlow knows because she witnessed it, but we don't talk about it. Not really. She respects my privacy, and I love her for that.

I'm exhausted. Beyond exhausted really. It's been a long couple of days, not to mention the months and months before that.

Has it really only been a few days since I left Atlantic City with Simon?

Taking my time, I wash my hair and body, letting the warm water soothe my achy muscles, and the Tylenol I took before closing myself off in the bathroom is working wonders on my head. I doubt that will last, but a girl can dream.

I didn't respond to Martina's texts, but I did forward them to Harlow so she could have Story start working her magic. With Nico in Italy, heading up that mission, Story is our only option for all the techy stuff. She's not as good as Nico, but she's close.

I'm not holding out hope though. Martina is clearly better

than both of them. She's stayed off the radar for years, despite her online presence. I don't know how she does it, and I suppose it doesn't matter.

When I turn the water off, the sound of voices filters in, and I strain to try and make them out. I hear Benson and Simon, but there's a third voice I don't recognize. And that makes me all sorts of twitchy.

I quickly dry off and throw on the clothes I set on top of the closed toilet lid. I slide my cell into my bra, some internal instinct screaming at me to keep it hidden, or as hidden as possible. After throwing my towel over the curtain rod to dry, I yank open the door and rush out to the living room. Benson and Simon are sitting at the kitchen table, and a man is sitting with his back to me.

He's questioning them about why they didn't call to inform him that Simon had been returned, and the more I hear him talk, the more the hair on my arms stand on end. I know that voice. But how? From where?

"Oh, hey, Marisol," Benson says as he stands. "Special Agent Calhoun stopped by to give us an update, but it seems we're giving him the update since…"

As if Benson weren't talking, the man stands and turns, and my vision blurs.

"Hello, Mari."

"Wait," Benson says, catching the name quickly. "Do you two know each other?"

"Benson, take Simon and get out of here," I say as calmly as I can. "Now."

"Marisol, what's—"

"Now!" I shout.

"I wouldn't do that if I were you," the agent says as he draws his weapon and trains it on Simon.

Simon clutches his dad's arm, fear filling his brown eyes.

"I thought you were dead," I say to the man.

"Death looks good on me, don't you think?"

"Never had you pegged for a G-man, Frank."

"Would someone please tell me what's going on?" Benson says as he urges Simon behind him.

"Are you really FBI, Frank, or is that a ruse?" I ask, ignoring Benson, knowing that I need to keep Frank's focus on me.

"Turns out, the FBI really sucks as weeding out the crazies," Frank says matter-of-factly. "Or maybe it's that everyone has a price. And me? Well, I've got a ton of fucking money."

"So, in summary, you are FBI, but you're still a scumbag?"

Frank shifts his gun in my direction. "I'd be careful, Mari. Martina said not to kill you, but I'm dangerously close to disobeying her."

"My name is Marisol," I snarl.

"Nah, I like Mari better."

"Mama," Simon cries from behind his dad. "Are you really, really mad?"

Ah, hell. Break my heart, why don't you?

"I'm getting there, little man," I assure him, hoping he understands.

"Marisol?" Benson prods, no doubt still wanting information.

"Frank here," I begin. "Is the man who bought Martina."

"How is that possible?"

"Anything is possible, Mr. Green," Frank says in an authoritative voice. "Anything at all."

"Look, Frank, take me," I plead, hating that I even have to. If he would just turn around for a second, I could lunge for my ax and give us a shot at getting out of here. "Martina doesn't really care about them. She wants to make me suffer for not joining her efforts."

"Yeah, no. I bought Simon fair and square, so I'm here to collect. Getting you for Martina is the icing on this delicious cake."

"Where is she, by the way?" I tilt my head. "I see she's not here to get her hands dirty."

"She's around," he says, but his eye twitches, giving me a glimpse of what his weakness is.

"Ah, so she sent you to do all the heavy lifting? Wow, I'm surprised you're going for that, Frank. Big, strong man like you? Surely you don't need to take orders from a little ol' female," I taunt.

Benson snorts, which garners Frank's attention, and gives me an opening. I dive for my bag, but rather than grab my ax, I grab the gun. Before Frank can even refocus on me, I'm lying on the floor, staring up at him, the barrel pointing at his face. I love my knife and ax, but I'm a damn good shot, too. As the enforcer, I've mastered every weapon I've been able to get my hands on.

"You wouldn't dare," Frank seethes.

"Wouldn't I?" I counter.

I know my aim is dead on, so I keep my eyes focused on his trigger finger. Even the slightest movement, and I'm putting a bullet in his ugly fucking face.

"You kill me, and she'll come for you," he says. "She'll never let you rest."

"I'm counting on it, *Agent*," I sneer.

Frank's finger moves, and I pull my trigger. Simon screams, and Benson tackles him to the ground and lays his body over his son's.

My bullet hits Frank dead center between his eyes, and the fucker manages to send his bullet through my arm. Frank falls, and I groan.

"Motherfucker."

"Mama!" Simon shouts. "Daddy, get Mama!"

I roll to my side, cradling my arm as blood oozes between my fingers, and force a smile.

"I'm okay, little man," I assure him as he and Benson crawl toward me. "I'm okay."

"He shot you," Benson growls and reaches for the blanket on the couch to press it to the wound.

"I shot him."

"How are you so calm?"

"Not the first time I've been shot and won't be the last."

"I don't want you to get shot anymore, Mama," Simon says, tears in his eyes.

"I know. And I'm really sorry you had to see that. But you were so brave."

"I was?"

"Yeah, little man. You really were. I'm proud of you."

The tears seem to vanish, and Simon beams. "You are?"

"Of course, I am. And I know your dad is too."

Simon looks at Benson. "You are?"

"I'm always proud of you, kiddo."

"Wow," Simon says with wonder. "I guess I'm a superhero too."

Benson and I exchange a look before breaking out into laughter. I just killed a man, and my arm hurts like a son of a bitch, but fuck does it feel good to laugh.

CHAPTER 18

Benson

"I'M REALLY SORRY."

I glance at Marisol, who's standing in my son's bedroom doorway, supervising as I help him pack a few bags. Her arm is wrapped in a sling, which she had in her vehicle. I asked her about it, but she just shook her head at me like I should've known she'd have medical supplies.

"It's not your fault," I tell her for what has to be the fifth time. "Besides, it's only for a few days, right?"

She lowers her gaze to the floor and swings one foot. "Right."

After we got her patched up, she called Harlow, who made some more calls, and my house is no longer the resting place for a corpse. Two men showed up, got the body, cleaned the floor disturbingly fast, and left. If it weren't for Marisol's sling, sullen attitude, and my memory, I'd never know that a murder took place a few hours ago.

I'm trying not to think about how calm I am about all of this, or how calm Simon is, but it's hard. If someone would have told me three days ago that this would be my life, I'd have smashed a liquor bottle over their head.

I could really go for a drink.

But as I stare at Marisol, I talk myself out of it. I'm shaky, yes, and it would help take the edge off, but I can't do that to her. Not now, not after what she did for me, for Simon. I'll suffer if it means making this even a fraction easier on her. I owe her that… at least.

"Do you really think we're safe making the drive to Atlantic City?" I ask as I join her near the door, out of Simon's earshot.

"Harlow will make sure we have an escort. If I have to guess, one of Malachi and Nico's teams are probably already stationed close. It's not a long drive as long as traffic isn't too bad."

"So it is safe?"

She smiles. "Yes, Benson. It's safe."

"Where do you think Martina is?"

Her face hardens. "I don't know, and that's the problem. She could be as close as the front porch, or as far as China."

"The front porch?"

"Bad example. Sorry."

"It's okay."

Marisol looks past me at Simon. "Almost done, little man?"

"Yeah." He glances over his shoulder at her. "Does Noah know I'm coming? Can I spend the night at his house tonight?"

"Woah, kiddo, slow your roll. Let's focus on getting out of here and on the road, then we can talk sleeping arrangements, okay?"

"But Dad, Noah probably misses me," Simon says with the assurance of a grown man. "He's gonna want me to stay at his house."

"He's not wrong," Marisol says. "He and Noah got along great."

"I just don't feel comfortable letting Simon out of my sight," I admit.

She rolls her eyes at me. "If Simon stays over with Noah, you and I will too. Giggles will insist on it. She does the same work I do, Benson. She's very aware of how important it will be for you to be close to Simon."

"Oh."

"I'm ready," Simon chirps as he drags two of his bags across the floor by the handles.

"Here, kiddo," I say as I rush to help him. "Head on out to the kitchen and grab a couple juice boxes out of the fridge. You can take them in the car."

"Or," Marisol begins, drawing out the word. "We could skip the juice boxes and stop for milkshakes on the way."

"Milkshakes!" Simons yells.

"Or we could do that," I capitulate. "But you also have to eat some fries and a burger, kiddo. You can't survive on milkshakes alone."

"Aw, Dad."

"Hey, that's Mama's rule, not mine."

Marisol smacks me on the arm. "Liar," she whispers.

I shrug.

"Fine, have it your way," she says with a wink. "We'll play by Mama's rules."

"Oh, Dad, get ready," Simon cheers. "Mama's rules for road trips are so much fun."

What the hell am I getting myself into?

Three hours, two milkshake stops, five burgers, and four rousing games of 'I spy' later, I have my answer. I don't know about fun, under the circumstances, but a road trip with Mama's rules certainly is entertaining.

"Home sweet home," Marisol says as she gets out of the passenger seat.

That was the one rule I fought. She wanted to drive, but I managed to talk her out of it. It's bad enough that I had to leave my Harley behind.

Simon gets out of his booster seat, which I was a little

shocked Marisol had in her vehicle, and exits out the back driver's side door.

"Hey, I thought we were going to Noah's," he complains.

"We are, little man," Marisol tells him. "Remember, when I called Giggles, she said they wouldn't be home until later. So we have to wait until she texts to let us know when we can come."

"Oh, yeah. I forgot."

"That's okay. It's been a pretty long day, kiddo," I say as I join them at the back of the car.

As if on cue, Simon yawns. "I'm not tired," he insists, and all I can do is shake my head and chuckle.

Marisol yawns next before laughing. "Yeah, me either."

"Mama!"

Marisol's face lights up and she skirts around me and rushes forward to throw her good arm around an older woman.

"Tahiti," she exclaims. "I didn't think you'd be here."

"When Harlow told me you were heading home today, I decided to stay. I wanted to lay my eyes on you myself."

"Well, I'm glad you did," Marisol tells her as she tugs the woman toward me. "Tahiti, this is Benson Green, Simon's dad. Benson, this is Tahiti, one of the OGs here at DHMC."

"OG means original gangster, Dad," Simon says helpfully.

"Thanks, kiddo."

"Nice to meet you," Tahiti says as she shakes my hand. "You've got a pretty amazing kid there. He was a treat to have with us last week."

"Thank you, ma'am."

Tahiti smacks my arm. "Call me ma'am again, and I'll be getting my ax."

"Right. Marisol did say something about all the women here being badasses."

"Marisol, is it?" Tahiti asks with a wink.

"Don't, T," Marisol warns. "I've already been through this with Prez. I'm not doing it with you too."

"I know," Tahiti says with a cackle. "She told us."

"Of course, she did. Is nothing sacred?"

"Mama, you should know better than that by now."

Simon tugs on my hand. "Why does it matter if you call Mama Marisol, Dad?"

"It doesn't, kiddo. They're just joking around with one another."

His brows knit as he shrugs. "Oh. Okay."

"C'mon on inside," Tahiti urges, linking her arm through mine. "Harlow and the others are dying to meet you. They only sent me out because they think, since I'm older than they are, I'll go easier on you." She leans in close. "Shows how much they know."

When we get inside, the place is crowded, but not overly so. Marisol introduces me to Harlow, Peppermint, Story, Spooks, Vinnie, Fox, Fiona, and two very scantily clad women named Tempe and Tonya. It crosses my mind that this isn't an environment I want my eight-year-old son in, but the thought quickly passes when I see how they all dote on him.

Besides, he was here for a week. There's no telling what he saw then, not to mention what he saw when he was held captive. If half-naked women treating him like a prince is the worst of it, I can live with that.

Katie girl, I hope you can too.

Within an hour, Marisol receives a text from Giggles, and we're settling in the car again to head to her house so Simon can see Noah.

CHAPTER 19

Mama

"I CAN'T BELIEVE you wouldn't let me drive."

I give Benson a side-eye glare and shake my head as I turn onto the road Giggles lives on. It took us five whole minutes to argue about who was going to drive the eight miles to Giggles' house.

"I let you drive from Philly," I remind him. "Be grateful."

It was great back at the clubhouse, seeing him with my family. They all seemed to really like him, which isn't surprising, and that put me in a mood I'm not overly familiar with. Being happy isn't my specialty. I like it, and it scares the hell out of me.

"You're in a mood," he observes.

At least I'm not really, really mad.

"Sorry. Just tired." I glance in the rearview mirror and smile. "Seems someone else is, too."

Benson looks over his shoulder and laughs at the way Simon's head lolls to the side as he sleeps.

"Are we close?" Benson asks. "Should I wake him up?"

"Yeah, go ahead. It's the last house on this block."

"Simon," he says as he reaches back and shakes his son's leg. "Wake up, kiddo."

Simon sits up straight so fast, I don't know how he doesn't have whiplash. "I'm not tired."

"Yeah, right."

"I'm not," Simon insists. "Are we there yet, Mama?"

I flip on my turn signal. "Pulling in the driveway now."

"Noah's gonna be so surprised to see me."

Noah knows we're coming, but I don't correct him. No sense in killing his joy.

After shifting into park and turning off the engine, I lean back against the seat. "I should warn you," I say to Benson. "Giggles is a very happy person."

"She really is, Dad," Simon agrees. "She's named Giggles because she giggles so much."

Benson grins. "Noted."

"And whatever you do, don't tease her about it. That makes her really, really mad," I tell him.

"Really, really mad, Dad," Simon laments.

"Okay. No teasing Giggles about her giggling. Got it."

After the warnings are complete, I lead them into the house, using the keypad to gain entry. None of us have key locks on our doors, as they're easy to pick. Keypads can be hacked, but it takes a bit longer with the system Nico set up for all of us.

"I need to do that at my house," Benson says. "Keep the crazies out."

"I'm going to pretend you didn't just say that," I comment. "And for the record, I didn't pick the lock. Simon let me in."

"You see it your way, and I see it mine."

Ignoring him, I close the door and set the lock. "Giggles, we're here," I call out.

I'm a little surprised Noah hasn't barreled us over to get to Simon, but it is late. Maybe Giggles has him set up with a movie or something.

"Hey, Mama," Giggles says as she walks around the

corner from where the kitchen is, and immediately, I can tell something is off. She's not bubbly or excited, and she's not even looking at Benson.

"Benson, I forgot my bag in the car," I say calmly, forcing a minimal amount of cheer into my tone. I don't know what's going on, but whatever it is, I don't want him or Simon here for it. "Can you grab it for me? And take Simon. He can help you carry the other bags."

"Don't fucking do it."

Shit.

Martina steps around the corner behind Giggles, a gun pointed at her head.

"Mari, really?" Martina says with a tilt of her head. "Always trying to save people."

"Someone has to," I snarl. "Especially with trash like you out there in the world."

"Watch it, little sister. You already killed my husband. I'm not feeling very forgiving right now."

"Husband?" Benson asks from beside me.

"Martina Calhoun. Special Agent Franklin Calhoun may have purchased me, but he won me over pretty quickly, so I married the son of a bitch," she says as she steps forward like she's the belle of some fucking ball. "Pleasure to meet you, Mr. Green."

Benson's eyes dart from my sister to me. "Is she for real?"

"Unfortunately." I glance at Giggles. "Where's Noah?"

Martina moves to the side so she can see both Giggles and me. "Yes, where is he? I'd love to get a good look at my future merchandise."

And that's another way to make Giggles really, really mad.

Giggles lunges toward the hall, where she has a small table with a false bottom that holds one of her many weapons. Martina pulls the trigger, and her shot goes wide, missing Giggles completely. She quickly takes another shot, before Giggles can get her hand on her own gun and hits her in the side. It all happens so fast that I don't have time to grab the knife I keep in my boot.

Dammit!

"Martina, stop!" I shout, trying not to crumble under the weight of potentially losing Giggles. "It's me you want."

"No, Mari," Martina sneers. "I want Simon. Hand him over, and I disappear."

"Fuck that," Benson growls. "You will not get my son."

"Oh, but Mr. Green, I already did."

"What happened to you?" I ask. "Seriously, Martina, what happened? Because you weren't always this vile."

"Life happened, Mari," she snaps. "It's a cruel, cruel world, or haven't you noticed?"

"And it's people like you that make it that way," I accuse. "I don't get it. We had a good childhood. We had parents who loved us. At least until you disappeared."

"Mama?" Simon says quietly. "Is she really your sister?"

"Yes, *Mama*. Answer the boy," Martina demands.

"Simon, I need you to listen to me very carefully, okay?"

"Okay."

"Blood isn't the only thing that makes a family," I explain. "And sometimes, it's exactly what rips a family apart."

"Oh."

"Giggles is my family, and Noah, and all the other women back at the clubhouse. They are my family," I say, my voice tight.

"Am I your family?" he asks.

Benson's sharp intake of breath cuts through the air, and I can only imagine what he's thinking.

"Yeah, little man, you are. The moment I carried you out of that building, you became my family. And I will do whatever it takes to protect my family."

"You're my family, too, Mama."

Man, this kid really knows how to gut-punch me… in a good way.

"Well isn't that sweet," Martina says mockingly as she lifts her gun and points it at me. "But how do you plan on protecting yourself, Mari?"

"Don't call me that," I snarl as I take a step forward. Benson reaches for my good arm, but I shake him off. "Don't you fucking dare call me that."

I take another step toward the barrel of Martina's gun. If she's going to kill anyone tonight, it's going to be me. I'll be damned if I let her take anything else from Benson and Simon. Those two have been through enough.

Movement catches my eye, but I don't let on that I notice. I can't afford to. Not if I'm going to maintain control of the situation.

"Hey, bitch," Giggles calls from the floor.

Martina turns, startled, which gives me the split-second I need to bend and grab my knife. But before I can do anything with it, Martina faces me again, so I slyly tuck it in my hand, blade up and hidden by my arm.

"What's going on?" she demands.

"You're awfully paranoid," I say as I take another step toward her.

"Stop, Mari. Stop whatever it is you're doing."

"That's rich," I snort. "I'm just standing here, trying to keep you from killing someone. You're the one with the gun."

"You always were such a smart ass." Martina waves the gun around absently. "But remember, Mari, this is your fault. You're the one who let me walk out that door years ago, and you're the one who took my property."

"I'm also the one who killed Frank," I taunt.

"I'm really enjoying this little family reunion," Giggles says, her words slurred from blood loss. "But can we mo—"

"Shut up!" Martina screams, her attention diverted from me.

"Finally," Benson mumbles as I lunge at Martina and thrust my knife into her stomach.

I yank the blade out, savoring the way Martina's eyes widen in shock. Lifting the blade over my head, I plunge it into her chest. Over and over again, I stab the woman who used to be family. And every single time the blade slices through her flesh and organs, my grin spreads.

I have always loved what I do, what the club does. But nothing has ever come close to the euphoria I feel at this moment.

"Mama!"

Arms wrap around me from behind, and I struggle against them, fighting to break free and continue my assault. Adrenaline courses through me, dulling the pain from my bullet wound.

"Marisol! That's enough."

Benson's deep voice breaks through, and I still in his arms.

"She's dead, Marisol. She's dead."

"Not dead enough," I pant. "I need to send her to Hell."

"No, you don't," Benson says, tightening his hold on me. "Her actions already paved the way."

"But—"

"Mama, please stop."

Fuck, that sweet voice.

My chest heaves as Benson slowly turns me around to face Simon. The boy is crying, but his shoulders are stiff as he does his best to be brave.

"Little man, come here," I say, holding my arms out for him. My sling is long gone, but even if it weren't, I'd always find a way to open my arms for my little man.

Simon throws himself at me, holding on tight, and we both fall to the floor. Benson lowers himself next to us, and Giggles crawls from across the room.

"I am so sorry," I murmur. "So damn sorry."

"It's okay, Mama. It's not your fault," Simon says. "She was a bad person. And you kept us safe, like you said you would."

"Out of the mouths of babes," Giggles mumbles.

"Shit." I pull away from Simon and look at Giggles. "Where's Noah?"

"He's fine. As soon as I pulled into the garage, my Spidey-senses started tingling so I sent him to the panic room."

"Oh, thank God."

"No, Marisol," Benson says, pulling me toward him and pressing a gentle kiss to my forehead. "Thank you."

Epilogue

BENSON

One year later…

"ARE YOU SURE ABOUT THIS?"

I pull Marisol into my arms and fuse my lips to hers. Kissing her breathless has quickly become my new favorite pastime.

"Aw, Dad, gross."

She pushes out of my hold and ruffles Simon's hair when he steps up next to us. "Get used to it, little man."

"Mama, I'm nine now. I think it's time you stop calling me 'little man'."

"I'll never stop calling you that."

Simon groans as he trudges out of the bedroom.

"I guess he didn't need anything important," Marisol says with a chuckle.

"If he did, he'll be back," I assure her.

Simon isn't ever too far away from me. After everything that went down with Frank and Martina, his nightmares got worse. I got him set up with a counselor as soon as we got back to Philly, and that had definitely helped. He's opened up to me a little about the six months he was held captive, but I don't push.

That's one thing I learned from my own therapy sessions. When my son is ready to talk, he will. In the meantime, showing him love and support is the best thing I can do.

Oh, and not drinking. Honestly, it was a lot easier to give that up than I thought it would be. When Marisol told me about her parents, it was like a switch flipped, and drinking just became something that wasn't important. I wanted to be present for my son in a way her parents weren't for her. And alcohol wouldn't allow me to do that.

"Benson, you didn't answer my question," she prods.

"Yes, I'm sure. I already have Simon signed up for school, and I start my new job next week. Couldn't really back out now even if I wanted."

Her face falls. "Do you want to?"

"Marisol, there is nowhere else I'd rather be than in Atlantic City with you and your crazy family. So no, I don't want to back out."

"I can't believe this is finally happening," she comments as she starts to tape up the boxes I've already packed. "I mean, we really didn't like each other there in the beginning."

Leaning into her neck, I lick a path up to her ear. "I liked some things," I whisper.

"Well, yeah, me too. But other than the sex, it was rough going."

"The sex was rough sometimes, too." I waggle my eyebrows at her.

"Stop it, Benson. You know what I mean."

I do. But I don't like to think about it. Not too much, anyway. Marisol and I were like oil and water when we first met. I wanted nothing to do with her. And even when feelings started to develop, I resisted.

For the first two months after she killed Martina, Simon and I returned to Philly, and I didn't hear from Marisol at all.

But then I caught Simon talking on the phone one night, and he admitted that he'd been secretly calling her before bed every night since we left the clubhouse.

After that, I joined in on the calls, and it became a bedtime ritual. Simon would take a bath, I'd tuck him in, and then we'd Facetime Marisol so she could tell him goodnight. After a few weeks of that, I started talking to her long after Simon fell asleep.

Then the weekend visits started, and before I knew what hit me, I realized I was falling in love with her. Maybe the love was always there, on some level. Love and hate are two sides to the same coin, after all.

"You got quiet," she observes.

"Just thinking."

"About?"

"You."

"All good thoughts, I hope."

"Always."

She snorts. "Did you lie to Katie too?"

That's one of the many things I love about Marisol. She doesn't shy away from talking about Katie. She knows I was married and lost a great love, and she respects that. She knows it's not a competition. Katie had my love and devotion, and now Marisol does. It's that simple.

And she insists on keeping Katie's memory alive for Simon. There are no words to express how grateful I am for that. I know Simon is too, even if he does act like a little shit sometimes.

"I don't lie," I insist.

"Uh huh." Marisol swats at my hands when I try to grab her by the waist. "I'll have to ask her next time we visit her grave."

"Like you'll get an answer."

"Benson, Katie talks to me all the time." I arch a brow, and she shrugs. "What? She does. And I talk to her... a lot.

Raising a boy is hard work. I need all the angelic help I can get."

"Have I told you lately how much I love you?"

She taps her chin and pretends to think about it. "Not in the last hour, at least."

When I reach for her this time, she doesn't swat me away. Instead, she wraps her arms around my waist.

"Well, I love you. So damn much."

"I love you too."

"Good." I give her a quick peck. "Now let's get to work. This shit isn't gonna pack or move on its own."

I swat her ass, and she laughs as she returns to taping boxes. Watching her for a minute, I silently talk to my late wife.

Katie girl, I promised. And I kept my promise. Simon is loved and happy. And so am I. I hope you know that.

If I believed in such things, I'd swear the wind carried her voice through the closed window so she could whisper in my ear.

I know, Benson. I will always love you, but you belong with her now. Goodbye, my love. Until we meet again.

If you enjoyed Mama's Rules and want to read more about the Atlantic City chapter of the Devil's Handmaidens MC, check out Harlow's Gamble:

HARLOW'S GAMBLE: BOOK #1

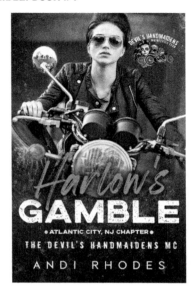

Harlow…

I was raised around pinging slot machines and the jubilant shouts of middle-aged women who won any amount of money at the Devil's Double Down casino. Beneath it all was the Devil's Handmaidens Motorcycle Club: Atlantic City, NJ chapter. I've grown from a fascinated little girl into the president of the MC, in charge of a thriving casino and underground business that no one knows about. Unless they've already proven their loyalty to me and DHMC. And I take my position of authority very seriously.

Unfortunately, we have competition in both businesses. Lots of competition. But only one of them is making it an issue and forcing me to take action. I have no problem doing whatever it takes to protect what's mine, but how am I supposed to do that when I'm battling insane attraction to their leader in the process?

Malachi...

There are two types of people in this world: leaders and followers. I'm a leader. It's something I've never questioned. Until the day I meet my match in a tiny spitfire full of threats and sinful beauty. She may run the competition for our casino, Umbria's Universe, but I still find myself wanting to follow her anywhere. Even when I should be putting as much distance between us as possible... or taking out her club entirely.

When our worlds collide in epic fashion, I'm forced to make a decision: continue to lead or start following. Both have their pros, and as much as I hate to admit it, leading has as many cons as following. I just need to figure out which is more acceptable. Because if ever there's someone who makes me want to compromise everything I've spent my life building, it's her. But between her smart mouth and violent actions, it's more than a little difficult to determine if she feels the same.

Prologue

HARLOW

Ten years ago…

"WE HAVE another winner here at the Devil's Double Down…"

I roll my eyes and ignore the rest of the announcement. I've heard it hundreds and hundreds of times in my life. When I was younger, I loved it. Loved the pinging of the machines, the way old ladies came in and lost their shit when they won any amount of money. It was fascinating to me.

But now I'm sixteen and there are more important things in life than bright lights and clanging machines. Like why my mom has me stuffed in this stupid room instead of watching her handle business. She's always told me that I'll take over one day: the casino, the club, the family. So it makes no sense to me why I'm stuck behind the glass of her upstairs office, watching everything from a distance.

"Club business" was the only answer she gave me when I asked her for an explanation. Oh yeah, did I mention my mom is the president of the Atlantic City, New Jersey chapter of an all-female motorcycle club? The Devil's Handmaidens MC to be exact. The baddest bitches in the state, in the country really, and I'm one of them. Or I will be someday, when I'm 'old enough' and 'ready'.

I flip my hatchet end over end as I stare at the blue-hairs below, my eyes tracking everything going on in the casino. I'm never without my hatchet. Unless I'm at school. Those pricks don't let us bring in anything fun.

Anyway, I'm babysitting. I'm fucking babysitting the casino. Mom tells me it's an important job, just as important, if not more, than anything else the club does. But all it is to me is a noose around my neck holding me back from doing what I really want to do. Be a part of real club business.

My lips tip up into a grin, but it quickly slips when I try to picture exactly what real club business looks like. Because the truth of the matter is, I don't know. I've grown up in the club, around the members and officers. I've been exposed to more than most young girls. And I've also been shielded, protected.

Lillith Monroe, aka Velvet, wanted her daughter to have a normal life, or as normal as possible under the club's wing. I was read bedtime stories, taken to the park, had tea parties, and played dress up. Granted, my tea parties and dress up consisted of leather and pretend liquor, but I was still allowed to be a little girl.

As I got older, my toys changed from dollhouses and tea sets to poker chips and hatchets. I no longer wanted to ride my Barbie bicycle because I wanted my two wheels to look like everyone else's: black and chrome with the Harley emblem proudly displayed. I didn't want to walk around the casino floor anymore and have my cheeks pinched by our customers. No, I wanted to be the one doing the pinching.

I glance at the steel blade with its custom wrapped leather handle in my hands, and my grin returns. Rising up from the worn-out chair that faces the glass overlook, I whirl around and launch my weapon at the target next to the door.

As it sails through the air, the door swings open, and I

squeal. The Sergeant at Arms of DHMC, Tahiti, cuts her gaze to the hatchet that missed her by inches.

"Fucking hell, Velvet needs to move this goddamn target before one of her own ends up dead," Tahiti says before turning to look at me, her hand still on the doorknob. "What's got you in a funk?"

I flop down into the chair and cross my arms over my chest, huffing out a breath in the process. "Babysitting."

Tahiti smiles a knowing smile. Bitch hates this post as much as I do. The difference is, she's not usually stuck with it because she's needed for club business.

"Two years, Har," she says, like she always does. "You've got two fucking years until you can prospect. Let's try to stay out of juvie until then, yeah?"

She reaches with her free arm and yanks the hatchet out of the wall. Her eyes rake over the sweet-sixteen gift my mom bought me two months ago. All the members were envious of the custom piece when I lifted it out of the box at my birthday party, and so far, Tahiti is the only one who hasn't gone out and purchased one for herself.

"Yeah, yeah," I grumble.

Tahiti stares at me for a moment before she grins. "Wanna get out of here?"

Immediately, I sit up a little straighter. "Do motorcycles have handlebars?"

Her spiky blonde hair doesn't move an inch as she throws her head back and laughs.

When she sobers, there's a fire in her eyes that wasn't there a second ago. "Seriously though, Velvet wanted me to come get you."

My excitement diminishes. "What's she need me to do now? Go take out the trash or something?"

"Or something." Tahiti thrusts the hatchet in my direction. "C'mon, Har. You're gonna need this."

I leap from the chair and cross the room as fast as I can,

taking my blade from her. If I'm gonna need this, it can't be something too bad, right?

I follow Tahiti down the hallway toward the back staircase, the one that leads to the basement of the casino. My heartbeat quickens the closer we get because I've never been allowed into the basement.

Calm down, Harlow. You might not be going all the way down.

"So, how's school going?" Tahiti asks as she pushes open the stairwell door.

"Eh."

She glances at me over her shoulder. "Oh, c'mon, Har. It can't be that bad."

I shrug. "It's school, T. Nothing special."

"Isn't the Spring dance coming up?"

I groan. "Next weekend."

"Got a date yet?"

"Hell no. I'm not going."

"Seriously?" She stops with her foot hovering above the next step and turns to face me. "Why?"

I lift my hatchet and smirk. "Not exactly a ton of guys lining up to ask me."

Tahiti shakes her head and grins. "They don't know what they're missing." Her eyes lower until she takes in my still growing cleavage, and then lower still to the shorts I'm wearing. "Not that you're trying to hide any of it."

"It's just a stupid dance, T. I don't wanna go anyway. I'd rather be at the clubhouse."

That's true, to a point. I love being at the clubhouse. And it *is* a stupid dance. But shit, I wanna go. Not alone, though.

"Whatever you say."

Tahiti doesn't push and continues down the steps. I try to suppress my shock when we pass the door for the first level, but it's impossible. The burst of air rushes past my lips, despite my pressing them together.

"Don't get too excited," Tahiti says over her shoulder. "Once you see what's down here, you can never unsee it."

There's something in her tone that causes my stomach to clench. Tahiti takes her job as SAA seriously, but nothing ever seems to phase her. But whatever we're walking toward, whatever is behind that all elusive door I've never been able to breach… it unnerves her, pulls her to a dark side she rarely displays around me.

When we reach the door, I stand next to Tahiti in the narrow hallway. She pulls her badge out from between her tits and holds it up to the lock pad. A soft beep fills the space around us, and the lock disengages as she tucks the card back into the safety of her double-Ds.

With both her hands on the door to push it open, Tahiti pauses and glances at me. "Brace yourself, Har."

And I do. Because the mixture of equal parts excitement and trepidation have me practically vibrating out of my skin. And if I'm being let in on whatever the hell this is, I have no time for giving in to either.

Tahiti pushes the door all the way open, and I'm greeted by a sight that will forever change my life. I don't know how, but I know it will. The sight will be emblazoned on my brain, in my soul, until I take my dying breath.

Because staring back at me, through the stink of desperation and suffering, are the eyes of dozens of girls—few appear older than me, but I'd bet my Harley savings that most are my age or younger—who look scared for their lives.

"What the fuck is going on?" I snap, stomping to my mom, who I spot next to a cot a few feet away.

"Club business, Har," she replies calmly, quietly.

I watch my mother's actions as she covers up a girl who can't be more than ten or eleven with a blanket. She brushes the girl's hair out of her face, like she used to do to me, and whispers, "You're safe now, sweetie. Close your eyes and try to rest."

Mom grabs me by the elbow and practically drags me to the side of the room. I look around until my eyes land on Tahiti, now standing by the exit, a jittery glint in her eyes.

"Harlow," Mom says, pulling my attention back to her. "I need you to stay here, with some of the members, and help with these girls."

"Where'd they come from, Mom? What's going on?"

Mom tips her head back and blows out a breath. When she brings her gaze back to me, her eyes soften. "I wanted to keep you away from this until you were eighteen, when you'd be at least old enough to prospect." She pauses, but I don't speak. Her eyes leave mine for a minute, maybe two, as she looks out over the rows of cots, all full. When she looks at me again, her eyes are hard. She's Velvet now, not Mom or Lillith. All Velvet. "These girls were being trafficked for sex."

I gasp. It's not like I didn't know the world was fucked up, or that things like this happened, but I never for a moment dreamed it was happening under our noses or at our doorstep. All that protection I had, I suppose.

"Okay."

"Tahiti and I, and a few others, need to go back out."

"But why?" I suddenly don't want her to leave. I want her to stay, with me, where she's safe.

Mom grips my shoulders. "Harlow, listen to me," she snaps. "I have to do what I have to do. And that means you need to step up now and help take care of these girls. I need you. *They* need you."

I swallow past the lump in my throat and nod. "Okay, Mom."

"Good."

She presses a kiss to my forehead, lingering a little too long, and my eyes close of their own accord. She hasn't done that in forever. This must be bad. She turns to walk away from me, but I grab her wrist to stop her.

"Can you at least tell me where you're going?" I ask, fearing I'll get the same stock answer I always do.

A grin appears on her face, one that promises pain and suffering for those who cross her. Velvet, president of the DHMC: Atlantic City, NJ chapter is on full display in that grin.

"To take out the fuckers we rescued them from," she says coldly, swinging her arm to indicate the room.

With that, she walks toward Tahiti, toward the path to justice. I watch her go, but when the sun bursts through the opening exit door, I call out to her.

"I love—"

The door slams shut in her and Tahiti's wake.

You.

About the Author

Andi Rhodes is an author whose passion is creating romance from chaos in all her books! She writes MC (motorcycle club) romance with a generous helping of suspense and doesn't shy away from the more difficult topics. Her books can be triggering for some so consider yourself warned. Andi also ensures each book ends with the couple getting their HEA! Most importantly, Andi is living her real life HEA with her husband and their boxers.

For access to release info and updates, be sure to visit Andi's website at www.andirhodes.com.

Also by Andi Rhodes

Broken Rebel Brotherhood

Broken Souls

Broken Innocence

Broken Boundaries

Broken Rebel Brotherhood: Complete Series Box set

Broken Rebel Brotherhood: Next Generation

Broken Hearts

Broken Wings

Broken Mind

Bastards and Badges

Stark Revenge

Slade's Fall

Jett's Guard

Soulless Kings MC

Fender

Joker

Piston

Greaser

Riker

Trainwreck

Squirrel

Gibson

Flash

Royal

Satan's Legacy MC

Snow's Angel

Toga's Demons

Magic's Torment

Duck's Salvation

Dip's Flame

Devil's Handmaidens MC

Harlow's Gamble

Peppermint's Twist

Mama's Rules

Valhalla Rising MC

Viking

Mayhem Makers

Forever Savage

Saints Purgatory MC

Unholy Soul

Printed in Great Britain
by Amazon

57130205R00078